KT-175-935

Smooth Justice

In Bloomsbury Magistrates' Court Donald Ferney, the stipendiary magistrate, reigned supreme. Ferney sought to acquire the public image of 'the kindly magistrate' and his remarks – even his judgements – were sometimes aimed at the local reporters present in court. But among those who knew him better, Mr Ferney was not loved. He had indeed made many enemies in all departments of his life, in particular among the permanent staff who served his court.

Mr Ferney receives some threatening letters. These arrive while he is hearing the case of a detective sergeant charged with corruption. Mr Ferney's responsibility in this case is to throw it out or commit it for trial at the Old Bailey. The anonymous letters suggest something very unpleasant will happen to him if he doesn't mend his ways. Yet they don't specify precisely why he is being threatened.

Here is a setting for a classical whodunnit: a man with power – and a number of enemies each of whom has a specific reason for wanting him dead. And indeed the story does take the form of a classical whodunnit, though nothing develops as it should, and many things are not what they seem.

Michael Underwood is an acknowledged craftsman of the crime novel. He has never written a better book than *Smooth Justice* with its convincing characters, its splendid detailed setting in a magistrates' court, and a plot guaranteed to fool anyone, although the clues are there.

by the same author

MURDER ON TRIAL
MURDER MADE ABSOLUTE
DEATH ON REMAND
FALSE WITNESS
LAWFUL PURSUIT
ARM OF THE LAW
CAUSE OF DEATH
DEATH BY MISADVENTURE
ADAM'S CASE
THE CASE AGAINST PHILLIP QUEST
GIRL FOUND DEAD
THE CRIME OF COLIN WISE
THE UNPROFESSIONAL SPY
THE ANXIOUS CONSPIRATOR
A CRIME APART
THE MAN WHO DIED ON FRIDAY
THE MAN WHO KILLED TOO SOON
THE SHADOW GAME
THE SILENT LIARS
SHEM'S DEMISE
A TROUT IN THE MILK
REWARD FOR A DEFECTOR
A PINCH OF SNUFF
THE JUROR
MENACES, MENACES
MURDER WITH MALICE
THE FATAL TRIP
CROOKED WOOD
ANYTHING BUT THE TRUTH

SMOOTH JUSTICE

Michael Underwood

BOOK CLUB ASSOCIATES
LONDON

© Michael Underwood 1979

All rights reserved. No part of this publication
may be reproduced or transmitted, in any form or
by any means, without permission.

This edition published 1979 by
BOOK CLUB ASSOCIATES
by arrangement with
MACMILLAN LONDON LIMITED

Printed in Great Britain by
THE ANCHOR PRESS LTD
Tiptree, Essex

Bound in Great Britain by
WM BRENDON & SON LTD
Tiptree, Essex

CHAPTER 1

'You've been a very naughty old man.'

Mr Ferney fixed the occupant of the dock with a stern look over the top of the half-spectacles which he wore principally as an imagined enhancement of his judicial presence. Abraham Chalk stared back, a sudden, crafty flicker of hope in his eyes, which grew as the magistrate went on.

'You deserve to go to prison and that's where I ought to send you. Nevertheless, I've decided to be merciful on this occasion. . . .'

'Bless you, your worship, you won't regret it,' Chalk broke in in a voice that a lifetime of hard drinking had made sound like gravel being sifted.

'I hope that's right. But let me give you a word of advice. Stay away from drink.' The defendant nodded vigorously as his rheumy old mind began to focus on how quickly he could be inside a pub. 'If you don't,' Mr Ferney continued, 'you'll soon be in trouble again and you'll know what to expect. Do you understand?'

The defendant had ceased to listen, but after being prodded by P.C. Shipling, the jailer, he managed a vague nod.

Mr Ferney sighed and gazed, as if for support, at the small cluster of people standing at the rear of the court in the space reserved for the public. Several of them were regulars who turned up daily to hear justice dispensed in Mr Ferney's court. Two of them now exchanged indulgent glances before giving the magistrate their accolade of beaming approval.

'Very well, see that you don't let me down,' Mr Ferney

went on in a brisker tone. 'You will be conditionally discharged. That means—'

'I know what it means, your worship,' the defendant said hastily, hoping to stem a further homily and so get to the pub that much sooner.

'I suppose you should do by now,' the magistrate remarked with a faint smile directed at the public. 'Don't let me see you back here again, because next time, should there be a next time, I certainly shan't be so merciful.'

Muttering obsequiously, Abraham Chalk vacated the dock and was escorted from court by P.C. Shipling.

'Don't push your luck too far, Chalky,' the jailer said amiably when they were in the passage leading to the receipt of custom. 'Next time you could be in front of Mr Stempel.'

The defendant's sly grin became a sudden snarl. 'He's a real bastard, Stempel. Mr Ferney's fairer than any of 'em. 'E understands us.'

P.C. Shipling reported the result of the case to his colleague holding the fort in the office, who raised a surprised eyebrow.

'I know,' Shipling said. Jerking his head back in the direction of the court he added, 'He's been flogging the kindly magistrate line for all he's worth this morning.'

This was a reference to the fact that, not long after his appointment, a newspaper had dubbed Mr Ferney 'the kindly magistrate', since when the tag had not only stuck, but been assiduously cultivated by the magistrate himself.

Chalky's had been the last case in the morning list and P.C. Shipling expected to find the courtroom empty when he returned a few minutes later to collect his papers. He thrust through the swing door humming to himself, but ceased abruptly when he saw that the magistrate was still on the bench. The acting chief clerk, Miss Purton, and the court inspector, Inspector Dibben, were also in their res-

6

pective seats. The fourth person was Reg Atkins, the usher, who was standing close to the witness box and staring at the magistrate with a stony expression.

'I'm sure you don't mean to distract the court,' Mr Ferney was saying, 'but you're constantly moving around unnecessarily and then when I do require your attention, you've either slipped out or you appear to be sunk in sleep. Do you think you could try and carry out your duties with a little more discretion and perhaps a little more concentration as well?'

Reg Atkins' eyes had become fixed on the coat of arms on the wall behind the magistrate's chair and his expression was masklike.

Mr Ferney pushed back his chair and got up. He walked toward the bench door and paused for the usher to open it for him. But Atkins never moved and, after a fractional pause, the magistrate opened it himself, only a sudden tightening of his jaw muscle indicating his displeasure. As soon as he had disappeared, Reg Atkins turned and left the court without a word.

'He's really got it in for poor old Reg, hasn't he?' P.C. Shipling observed to the other two.

Miss Purton pursed her lips. 'He's trying to get him prematurely retired,' she said.

'Poor old Reg, he's been at this court a darned sight longer than Ferney,' Inspector Dibben remarked. 'Why can't he be left in peace? He's only got two years to go.'

'He's been here thirty-three years,' Miss Purton said.

'And Mr Ferney's only been a magistrate for four,' P.C. Shipling observed. After a pause he added, 'At least he didn't bawl him out in public this time like he did a couple of weeks ago. Reg took that pretty badly.'

'I'm not surprised,' Inspector Dibben said angrily. 'He was publicly humiliated. Held up to public ridicule, he

7

was.' He made a contemptuous sound. 'Kindly magistrate, indeed!'

Miss Purton rose, but refrained from adding any comment of her own. 'It's the Wilkley case all this afternoon,' she observed, as if nothing further need be said, which was near enough the truth.

Detective Sergeant Wilkley was appearing in Bloomsbury Magistrates' Court on a charge of corruption. He was an ex-officer of the Yard Vice Squad and had been suspended from duty for several months while the allegation of corruption had been under investigation. It had been an enquiry of endless ramifications and the present charge against him represented only the tip of the iceberg. The chief prosecution witness was a Soho criminal named Tremler who had made his accusation of bribery while himself serving a prison sentence. If the prosecution established a *prima facie* case, Sergeant Wilkley would be committed for trial at the Old Bailey. But he was fighting hard in the lower court and Mr Ferney, to the dismay of the investigating officer, had on at least one occasion shown himself hostile to their cause. Equally, it had to be said that he had taken every opportunity of harassing Mr Smeech, the defending solicitor, who was the principal in the firm of Smeech and Co. and who had the busiest solicitor's practice at the court, his office being just across the road. Mr Ferney had made it clear from his first arrival that merely because he appeared so frequently, Philip Smeech need not expect to receive any preferential treatment in his court. He underlined his determination not to accord him any, moreover, by faulting him on every possible occasion and treating him generally as a Victorian duke might his second footman.

The first thing that Donald Ferney did on reaching his room on the first floor of the court building was to take his brush and comb from the cupboard and attend to his hair, though his morning in court had done little to disturb it. It was still a good head of hair for a man of forty-six, thick and dark apart from a few touches of grey at the sides. There was one lock which was apt to descend over his forehead and he combed it vigorously back into place. It always fretted him when it fell forward, as he felt it detracted from his judicial persona. Satisfied that his hair was once more tidy, he picked up the clothes brush and fastidiously brushed the collar and shoulders of his jacket. He invariably wore a dark suit in court with a white shirt and a stiff white collar. At least *he* could never be accused of the slack sartorial standards found amongst so many of today's legal profession. Some of his colleagues on the metropolitan stipendiary bench actually wore suede shoes which he regarded as the ultimate in sloppiness. The toe-caps of his own highly polished black leather shoes always shone like nuggets of anthracite.

He replaced the brushes in their corner cupboard and gave himself an approving look in the mirror which hung on its door. His mind turned to his latest contretemps with Atkins. He really must persuade the powers that be to move him. It wasn't just that he was beyond the job, it was his attitude which bordered on the insolent. He seemed to have no respect for the dignity of the bench and then there had been that business of his using the magistrate's private entrance when he left to go home in the evening. Mr Ferney had caught him at it and told Miss Purton to tick him off. The reply had come back that he only used it when it was raining because it was nearer to the Underground station than the main door at the front of the court building. Since then Mr Ferney had good reason to believe that the usher had continued to use it whenever it suited him.

It was obvious that Miss Purton was unable to maintain discipline amongst the staff. Not that that really surprised him for she had revealed a number of shortcomings as acting chief clerk. The trouble was that too many of the staff had been there too long. A new broom had been overdue when he took up his appointment and he blamed himself for not having swept cleaner and quicker. Not that it was all that easy in these bureaucratic days, when trying to get rid of a civil servant was like pushing a boulder uphill.

Mr Ferney walked across to his desk and sat down. It was one of his lunchless days and he would spend the break re-reading his *Times* and tackling the crossword. The court matron would bring him a cup of coffee later on.

He was about to pick up the paper when he noticed a letter. It must have arrived in the course of the morning. There was nothing about the envelope to arouse his suspicion and he reached for a small ivory paperknife. The envelope bore his name and had 'personal' written in the top left-hand corner. But judges and magistrates often received letters marked 'private' or 'personal'. It was the sender's way of trying to ensure they reached their intended recipient and weren't opened by a clerk.

As he inserted the paperknife under the flap, he noticed that the envelope bore a 'London W.C.' postmark which was the postal area of the court. Inside was a folded sheet of paper which didn't match the blue envelope and his heart gave a slight jump, as he became almost certain it was another threatening letter. The first had arrived about ten days previously just after he had begun hearing the Wilkley case, not that it referred to that or any other case. But Detective Superintendent Evesham, who was the officer in charge of the Wilkley case and to whom he had shown the letter, thought it more than likely that its receipt and the start of the court proceedings against Detective Sergeant Wilkley were connected. He had suggested that Mr Ferney should not mention the letter to anyone and, in the meantime, he would begin some discreet enquiries.

Since when Mr Ferney had heard nothing further and had gone some way to putting the letter out of his mind.

But now he recalled its terms all too clearly. The threats had been imprecise, but had none the less hinted that a disagreeable end awaited him. Like all judicial officers he was used to receiving letters from cranks couched in aggressive and often obscene language, vilifying him for some decision or other taken in a case, but there had been something different about this letter. Hence he had shown it to Detective Superintendent Evesham who had agreed that it ought to be taken seriously.

In the first place the sender had gone to the trouble of composing it in words and letters cut from a newspaper and gummed to a sheet of paper. The appearance was messy, but the meaning was clear enough. It had been unsigned and the writing on the envelope had been different from that on the one he now held in his hand. Moreover, the first letter had come in a square white envelope as opposed to a rectangular blue one such as he now stared at.

Slowly, he extracted the sheet of paper and unfolded it, holding it carefully by his fingertips. Once again the text was composed of words and letters cut from a newspaper and gummed haphazardly to the paper. It was the familiar gum stains appearing on the reverse side that had alerted him as soon as he saw inside the envelope.

He laid the sheet of paper on the desk and stared at the ill-spaced words which ran across the centre.

'One, two, three and then you snuff it, Ferney.'

He stared at the brutally succinct message for half a minute, noticing that the words had all been cut out complete apart from 'Ferney' which had been painstakingly composed letter by letter. His expression was a mixture of fear and distaste as his eyes became riveted to the last five words. 'Snuff it' could have only one meaning and he gave a small shiver. He was still staring at it when there was a knock on his door and Elsie, the matron, entered with his cup of coffee. He slid his newspaper quickly over the letter so that she wouldn't see it.

'Tell P.C. Shipling I want to see him, will you?' he said as she turned to leave.

'What now, sir, or when he's finished his lunch?'

'Now.'

'Typical,' Elsie reflected as she made her way back to her domain next to the jailer's office. The same thought was in P.C. Shipling's mind as he reluctantly put down a half-eaten sandwich and began to do up the buttons of his jacket.

He paused outside the magistrate's door before giving it a brisk military rap. Mr Ferney looked up as he entered.

'Is Detective Superintendent Evesham here yet?' he asked.

'It's only half past one, sir. He doesn't usually come until about ten to two. Unless you asked him to be here earlier?'

Mr Ferney shook his head impatiently. 'I just thought he might have arrived.'

P.C. Shipling silently wondered exactly why the magistrate should expect busy police officers to arrive at his court before they had to.

'When he does come,' Mr Ferney went on, 'tell him I want to see him in my room before the court sits.'

'Yes, sir.'

P.C. Shipling hovered for a moment, waiting to see if there was more to follow. Nothing had been said which couldn't have been communicated on the internal phone. But then the magistrate liked to have the court staff at his beck and call.

'That's all, Shipling.'

P.C. Shipling returned downstairs to his half-eaten sandwich. He was an equable man and though the magistrate was a long way from being his favourite person, he had no reason to bear him the sort of resentment that some of the other staff did.

'Anyone would think we're his personal slaves,' Elsie said when he told her why he had been sent for.

P.C. Shipling laughed tolerantly. 'I reckon you need a special brand of humility not to let the job turn your head. Judges have juries to remind them that they can't get away with everything, but stipes can stalk about their backyards like randy cockerels. Anyway, there've been worse than D.F.'

'All I can say is that I wish we still had Mr Butterwick,' Elsie said with a sniff. 'There was a real gent for you.'

'*He* could be a sod in court at times.'

'He was always a gent to me.'

P.C. Shipling turned away to hide a smile. Elsie had always been sensitive to teasing about her alleged crush on Mr Ferney's predecessor.

'Hello, Jock, how are things in your powerhouse today?'

P.C. Shipling turned to find that Dectective Superintendent Evesham had come into the office.

'Ah, I'm glad you're here, guvnor. The magistrate wants to see you in his room.'

'What, now?'

'As soon as you arrived. You know your way up?'

Evesham nodded. 'Know what it's about?'

'He'd hardly tell the likes of me, guv.'

Evesham shrugged. 'O.K., I'll go and see what he wants.' In fact, he had little doubt that it concerned the threatening letter the magistrate had received the previous week. So far, his enquiries had produced nothing concrete, though he had discovered through the grapevine a surprising number of people who bore grudges of one sort or another against Mr Ferney. He had no intention of divulging this to the magistrate for the time being and, anyway, he was still inclined to think that the threats were linked to the Wilkley case.

'I'll let him know on the blower that you're on your way up,' P.C. Shipling said.

'Any chance of a cup of tea when I come back, Elsie?' Evesham asked, as he turned to go. 'I've come straight here from the Bailey and haven't had anything.'

'You're welcome any time, sir.'

Tom Evesham gave her a broad smile and departed. He was a shortish man of neat appearance and mild expression. He had had a rapid rise in the force and wouldn't be forty for another six months. His number two on the Wilkley enquiry, Detective Inspector Venyon, was by contrast a fast talker who impressed by his assertive manner. But anyone who believed that Evesham lived in his sidekick's shadow deceived himself.

'I understand you wanted to see me, sir,' he said, as he entered the magistrate's room after a brief knock on the door.

Mr Ferney, who hadn't heard the knock, looked up with a startled expression. He seemed on the verge of reproving his visitor, but, instead, held out the letter which he fished from beneath his *Times*.

'When did you receive this, sir?' Evesham asked, putting it down on the edge of the desk after reading it.

'This morning. It was here when I adjourned for lunch.'

'Have you told anyone about it?'

'No one.'

'Or about the other one?'

'No one. I've not mentioned it to a soul.'

Superintendent Evesham was thoughtful while the magistrate stared at him with a faintly impatient expression.

'Well, what have you been able to find out?' he asked tetchily when Evesham remained silent.

'Nothing as yet, I'm afraid, sir.'

'You still think these threats are in some way linked to the Wilkley case?'

'It seems more than a coincidence, sir, that this second letter arrives on the day the hearing resumes.'

'Well, whoever's sending them is very mistaken if he thinks I can be frightened off doing my duty,' Mr Ferney said stiffly. 'What do you think the one, two, three means?'

'That you'll receive three letters before any other move is made. Could be that!'

'So there's one more to come?'

'Yes.'

'After that, I shall be snuffed out?' Mr Ferney's tone was brittle.

'That's what it says, but it doesn't necessarily mean it.'

'Who are you to say that, if I may ask?'

'If the sender really meant business, he'd be unlikely to warn you in advance. He'd already have done what he intended doing. These letters are clearly meant to frighten you.'

'It takes more than a few childish threats to frighten me.'

Nevertheless, you're frightened, Evesham thought to himself. His guess was that the third letter would contain a specific demand either relating to the Wilkley case, or, if he was wrong about that, to some other matter. Either way, it would reveal its author's real motive. The first two letters could be seen as softening up the victim so that he was more likely to yield when the ultimatum came.

'We could arrange some form of police protection if you'd feel happier,' Evesham said. 'There's not much one can do, but I can have someone from your local station keep an eye on your house. I could probably also arrange for a police car to bring you to court in the morning and deliver you home in the evening.'

'That's a matter for you, Superintendent. If you think my life is seriously in danger, then it's obviously your duty to take the necessary steps. But don't put the onus on me. I'm not requesting police protection. Personally, I'm inclined to believe that these two letters are the work of some crank and have nothing to do with the Wilkley case at all. If they had, I can't see why they haven't said so. Anyway, the last thing I want is to go riding about in police cars. I've always been very careful not to give the impression of living in the pocket of the police. As far as I'm concerned, police witnesses have no monopoly of the truth in my court, as so many of them seem to think they have.'

Evesham had listened with an expression of polite attention. 'We won't do anything for the time being then, sir. The last thing I'd want to do is to cause you embarrassment and I certainly don't take these letters so seriously as to regard police protection as imperative.' He paused. 'When we spoke last week, sir, I did ask you to let me know if you could think of anyone who might bear you a grudge. Have you been able to give that matter some thought?'

Mr Ferney frowned. 'One is obviously a target for grudges if one does one's job conscientiously,' he said in a pompous tone. With a condescending smile, he went on, 'Unfortunately a magistrate cannot hope to please all the people all the time. There are always some people who refuse to recognise that justice has been done, if it isn't to their personal liking.' He shifted slightly in his chair as if he'd had a sudden sciatic spasm. 'About a month ago, I had a fellow called Alfred Turner in front of me. He was charged with assaulting someone in a bus queue. He was a complete rogue with a number of convictions though he had never actually been to prison. Anyway, that was where I sent him for six months and where he richly deserved to go. When he'd recovered from his shock on being sentenced, he shouted threats at me before the jailer could get him out of court. Shipling was clearly taken by surprise and there was a bit of a struggle before Turner was removed.'

'What sort of threats were they?'

'His were nothing more than general abuse, but his common law wife – a real harridan – was in the public gallery and shouted out that she'd "get me" and see me suffer for what I'd done to her so-called husband.' He glanced up at Evesham. 'She's the only person I've been able to think of who might have sent the letters. She was obviously the sort of vindictive and vicious woman capable of such action.'

'I can doubtless get Turner's address from the office downstairs,' Evesham observed mildly. 'I take it, sir, you didn't take the threats particularly seriously at the time.'

'Never gave them another thought until you asked me to rack my brains.'

'Any other ideas?'

Mr Ferney shook his head. 'I'm afraid not.'

Superintendent Evesham was silent for a time. Then he said quietly, 'I gather, sir, that you've been having a bit of bother with Atkins, the usher.'

Mr Ferney looked annoyed. 'Atkins is no longer up to the job, but like a lot of old men, he's thoroughly stubborn and doesn't like being told anything. He may be tiresome and stupid, but I don't see him as the author of those letters. After all, he's still got his pension to think about.'

Evesham nodded and glanced round the room. 'Would he have occasion to come up here?'

'Indeed, yes. He escorts me down to court. Also, part of our quarrel has been over his use of the magistrate's private entrance for going home. No one is supposed to use that door save myself or a colleague. Only I and my fellow magistrate have a key to it, but that doesn't prevent Atkins going out that way, even though he can't get in.'

This tallied with what Evesham had heard through the

grapevine. He would take an opportunity of studying Reg Atkins when they were all in court this afternoon.

'Well, sir, if you've nothing else to tell me, I'd better go downstairs and make sure everything's ready.' He glanced at his watch. 'What time will you be sitting?'

'I'll say a quarter past two . . .'

There was a peremptory knock on the door which was flung open to reveal Reg Atkins gowned and glowering.

'Come back in ten minutes,' Mr Ferney said.

'It's nearly five past two now.'

'I'm well aware of that, but I shan't be sitting until a quarter past.'

Atkins sniffed and looked as if he was going to spit out the invisible raspberry pip on which his dentures never ceased working. Instead, however, he relieved his feelings by slamming the door.

'You see? He's quite impossible,' Mr Ferney remarked. 'A thoroughly cantankerous old man.'

Detective Superintendent Evesham smiled non-committally as he made his own departure from the magistrate's room.

It did now occur to him, however, that if the usher could be as rude as that to the magistrate's face, he would be quite capable of sending him anonymous threatening letters.

But through discreet enquiries he had learnt of two others on the court staff who might feel as strongly about Mr Ferney as Reg Atkins. First there was Miss Purton, on whom the magistrate had made an adverse report with the result that her confirmation in the post of chief clerk had been held up. She had, Evesham gathered, applied for a transfer to another court, but for various administrative reasons there was no prospect of this in the near future. Mr Ferney hadn't mentioned Miss Purton as someone who might bear him a grudge though he must be aware of her sense of grievance. Women of Miss Purton's age could behave unpredictably and, perhaps, he ought to find out something about her present circumstances. The one thing he had learnt as a police officer was never to be surprised by the most unlikely human behaviour. He had come across an eminent doctor who had relentlessly hounded his secretary because he believed she had fiddled the stamp money to the sum of 21p. He would ring her up in the middle of the night and try to extract a confession from her. And then there had been the archdeacon who would change into old clothes and go off anonymously to a large bingo hall once a week where, from all accounts, he played with fanatical zeal. Until one day he was caught cheating and asked not to come again.

But more interesting in a way than Miss Purton was Inspector Dibben. This was something Superintendent Evesham had learnt by chance from a colleague at the Yard. It appeared that about seven years previously Detective Sergeant Dibben, as he then was, had had a complaint made against him by Mr Ferney who was a member of the Bar at the time. It arose in the course of a case in which Mr Ferney was defending and Sergeant Dibben was the officer in charge. As a result of the complaint Sergeant Dibben had been transferred from the C.I.D. to the uniformed branch and his promotion had been delayed. It must have come as a disagreeable shock to him when Mr Ferney was appointed to Bloomsbury Magistrates' Court.

But if Miss Purton or Inspector Dibben had sent the letters, why had they waited until now? It was with this thought in his mind that he made his way back to the jailer's office and the cup of tea which Elsie had promised him.

On his way he crossed the vestibule of the court which was thronged with an assortment of people with an interest in the afternoon's case. Over in a corner conversing with his solicitor was Detective Sergeant Wilkley. On seeing

Evesham, he quickly looked away. He was a strapping man in his mid-thirties with hair brushed straight back from a broad forehead. An otherwise open countenance was negated by his eyes, which were small and heartless. From his enquiries, Evesham had no doubt that Sergeant Wilkley was an evil man, who had gone in for wholesale corruption in the sale of the favours he had to offer as a Vice Squad officer. In his case it had not been a question of waiting for a bribe to be offered, he had shown the ruthlessness and aggression of a high-powered salesman. Arms had been twisted until they snapped.

Detective Inspector Venyon was in the jailer's office when Evesham reached it.

'We're all ready, guv,' he said, with the air of a satisfied impresario.

'I didn't see Tremler when I passed through the vestibule just now.'

'I've got him tucked away in the café next door with Sergeant Smythe. Didn't want him to get first-night nerves hanging about outside the court. Sylvie's come, too.'

'As nurse companion?'

'I still think she ought to be called.'

Sylvie was Ralph Tremler's wife, a well-cushioned blonde who was reputed to be made of steel inside.

'And guess who else?' Inspector Venyon went on.

'Who?'

'Ruby.'

'Reuben Huxey?'

'His beautiful self.'

'Well, for heaven's sake don't let him get inside the court, Wally. I don't want that great ape's face anywhere around.'

Reuben Huxey was a deaf mute who had been in Tremler's employ for a dozen years. He was as strong as an ox and looked as if he'd emerged straight from Dr Frankenstein's laboratory. It was primarily on his account that Ralph Tremler seldom had trouble in his business deals. They went through without any of the usual haggling with Ruby's unseen presence looming over his employer's associates and competitors in the small Soho jungle.

'Don't worry, guvnor, he'll stay out of sight. I don't know why the hell Ralph let him come along.'

'I suppose he wanted all the support he could muster. I know he's not looking forward to giving evidence.'

'He won't let us down.'

'I bloody well hope not. But he's going to have to manage without Ruby's moral support. Having him in court would be like letting a hairless King Kong loose in Piccadilly.'

Evesham swallowed the remains of his tea, glanced at his watch and headed for court. Most of the leading players were already there, waiting for the magistrate's arrival. He smiled at Mr Jude who was prosecuting and gave a friendly nod at Philip Smeech, the defending solicitor.

A few moments later, the bench door opened and Reg Atkins came through and called out, 'Silence in court. All stand.' He moved aside to let the magistrate pass and then waited to close the door again with an air of ill-concealed impatience.

Mr Ferney reached his seat and turned to bow to the court. Before sitting down he let his gaze roam round like a sovereign's during the playing of the national anthem.

'Yes, Mr Jude,' he said to prosecuting counsel when he was satisfied that he had everyone's attention. 'Are you ready to start calling your evidence?'

Before Jude could stand up, however, Mr Smeech was on his feet.

'I have an application to make, sir. I shall be grateful if you will allow my client to sit beside me here rather than in the dock . . .'

'Why?'

'Because it will save me having to turn round and lean across every time I wish to speak to him. He's not in custody and therefore there wouldn't seem to be any objection, sir. Moreover, it's quite a normal practice.'

'I'd have thought it was for me to say whether there was any objection, Mr Smeech,' Mr Ferney said coldly. 'Moreover, I'm not concerned with what goes on in other courts. However, if it will obviate constant movement on your part, I'm prepared to allow it in the interests of quietness.'

'I'm much obliged, sir,' Smeech said with a sardonic edge to his tone.

The magistrate now turned toward prosecuting counsel again and Jude rose to his feet.

'I call Ralph Tremler.'

Detective Inspector Venyon who had been hovering near the door, opened it and beckoned to the witness whom he had stationed outside. As Tremler came through, Venyon pointed the way to the witness box.

Ralph Tremler was wearing a camel hair coat over a pale blue suit. His shirt was white silk and his tie a delicate pink. He was a short, swarthy man with a melancholy expression. His voice was so soft that Mr Ferney ordered him to speak up and to take the oath again. He wasn't much louder the second time. As he laid down the testament he glanced at Sergeant Wilkley sitting only a few feet away. Their eyes met like those of two cats in someone else's garden. It was anyone's guess what each was thinking.

'Is your name Ralph Tremler?' Mr Jude asked.

'Yes.'

'Where do you live?'

'In North London.'

'What address?'

'Finchley direction.'

'Will you tell the court the address?'

'I'd sooner not.'

'Why not?'

'It can bring aggro.'

'Perhaps the witness may be allowed to write his address down, sir?' Mr Jude said, turning toward Mr Ferney.

'What sort of aggro are you referring to?' the magistrate asked with a frown.

'If it gets out in the papers where I live, it can cause trouble.'

'Are you suggesting that you have enemies?'

'Certainly I have.'

Mr Ferney pursed his lips. 'I don't really approve, but I'll allow it on this occasion.'

Miss Purton, who was poised to record the witness's deposition, held out a piece of paper for Reg Atkins to give Tremler.

'Usher!' Mr Ferney said sharply, when it was apparent that Atkins' attention was elsewhere. 'Hand the witness that piece of paper.'

Meanwhile Jude waited patiently to get on with his examination-in-chief. If only court hearings were conducted with the speed they were given on television. No false starts and meanderings there. When he was able to continue, he asked, 'Do you know the defendant?'

'Yes.'

'How long have you known him?'

'Quite a few years.'

'How many?'

'About five.'

'How did you first come to meet him?'

'He raided my shop in Old Compton Street.'

'What sort of shop was it?'

'Books and magazines.'

'Pornographic?'

'If you like.'

'Does that mean yes?'

'Yes.'

'And after that?'

'He often used to drop by.'

'For what purpose?'

'Look around, have a chat.'

'Anything else?'

'Collect.'

'Collect what?'

'Money.'

'Tell us about that.'

'I gave him fifty quid a week.'

'For what purpose?'

'He'd tip me off about things.'

'What things?'

'What his lot were up to.'

'By "lot", do you mean the police?'

'Yes.'

'And what do you mean by "up to"?'

'You know.'

'Maybe I do, Mr Tremler, but your evidence is being written down and the learned clerk can only record what you say, not what she thinks you mean.'

'Mr Jude,' the magistrate broke in, 'it isn't only the clerk who matters, *I* also have to understand.'

'I certainly never intended to imply otherwise, sir. I apologise.'

Mr Ferney turned toward the witness. 'Do you think you could try and make your evidence less cryptic, Mr Tremler?'

The witness appeared to consider the request before giving a little shrug which could equally well have signified acquiescence or incomprehension of the question.

'You said in answer to my question that you paid the defendant fifty pounds a week to let you know what the police were up to,' Jude went on. 'What did you mean by "up to"?'

'Whose premises were going to get a going over.'

' "Going over"?'

'Searched,' the witness said wearily.

'You mean searched by virtue of a warrant under the Obscene Publications Act?'

'What else?'

'And have their stock seized?'

'They'd take the bible if it was there,' Tremler said in a tone of disgust.

'How long did you continue paying the defendant fifty pounds a week?'

'About six months.'

'What brought the arrangement to an end?'

'I was knocked off, wasn't I? Went inside for a year.'

'For what offence?'

'Selling books.'

'Obscene books?'

'What's obscene and what isn't? Nobody can tell you. It's all in the eye of the beholder, I says.'

'Anyway, it was an offence under the obscenity laws that got you sent to prison?'

'Yes.'

'And while you were in prison, you wrote to the Commissioner of Police about Detective Sergeant Wilkley?'

'Yes. If he hadn't double-crossed me, I wouldn't have been inside.'

'In what way did he double-cross you?'

For the first time, the witness's tone rang with emotion. 'Dropped me in the cart,' he said indignantly.

'Why should he have done that?'

'Because I refused to give him more money.'

'Did he ask for more?'

'A hundred.'

'A week?'

'Yes.'

'How soon after you refused his new demand were you arrested?'

'A couple of weeks later.'

'And it was because of the way he'd treated you that you made a complaint to the Commissioner?'

'Yes.'

'And did Detective Superintendent Evesham visit you in prison and take a statement from you?'

'That's right.'

'When was that?'

'About a year ago.'

'How long have you been out of prison?'

'Five months.'

Mr Jude looked across at Evesham, who gave him a small nod to indicate that he didn't think counsel had omitted anything. Prosecuting counsel then sat down.

'Where's the usher?' Mr Ferney said in the silence that followed.

'He's just slipped out of court, sir,' Inspector Dibben replied, half-rising in his seat. 'He'll be back in a moment.'

Mr Ferney rolled his eyes heavenwards with an expression of long-suffering. 'When he returns, will you tell him to close that window at the rear of the court. I can see there's a terrible draught coming through which can't be very pleasant for those in the public gallery. I don't want them all going down with colds or stiff necks.' As he finished speaking, he glanced towards the row of reporters on the press bench. Three of them had no interest in Mr Ferney or his court beyond the case in hand. The fourth, however, was a regular who dutifully took down the magistrate's words for the local paper, *The Bloomsbury and Holborn Gazette*. It was the readers of this weekly journal

26

who were constantly reminded of the benign and humane justice administered in their area.

Mr Ferney now glanced at Philip Smeech.

'Do you wish to cross-examine?' he asked in a not particularly friendly tone.

'Yes, sir.'

'You will bear in mind, won't you, that I'm not trying this case? I'm merely here to decide whether there's a *prima facie* case justifying a committal for trial at the Old Bailey. I hope you'll remember that.'

Philip Smeech swallowed the insult and said nothing. He was used to magistrates who regarded cross-examination as a waste of their time in cases destined for trial in a higher court. But he was not going to allow himself to be intimidated by Donald Ferney. He didn't enjoy having a running battle with the magistrate, but duty to his client came first and Detective Sergeant Wilkley had made it clear that he wanted the case fought hard and, if possible, knocked out in the magistrates' court.

When the solicitor acknowledged the admonition with no more than a cursory nod, Mr Ferney leaned back in his chair and closed his eyes.

'Is this the first time in your life you've ever given evidence for the prosecution?' Smeech asked.

'Yes.'

'Quite a novel experience for you?'

'Mr Smeech,' the magistrate interrupted, 'surely I don't have to tell *you* that questions and comments are two quite different things. More time is wasted in this court by advocates transgressing the rules of evidence than in any other way.'

'Even than by magisterial interruptions?' Smeech wanted to say, but didn't.

'How long had you been in prison before you decided to write to the Commissioner?'

'I can't remember.'

'Try.'

'A few weeks maybe.'

'Why did you wait?'

'I wanted to think.'

'What about?'

'Whether to tell what I knew.'

'Why did it require weeks of thought?'

'It was a serious matter.'

'Indeed, very serious for my client, but why wait before making this grave allegation of corruption?'

'I tell you, I wanted to think.'

'You weighed the matter up very carefully, is that what you're saying?'

'Yes.'

'But why if your story's true; why not report it at the first opportunity?'

'I didn't want to be hasty about it.'

'No one could accuse you of that. Isn't the real answer that your allegation is a complete concoction?'

'It happened like I've said.'

'I gather you were quite happy to pay my client fifty pounds a week?'

'Who's happy paying out money?'

'But you were getting a return, if you're to be believed?'

'It was sort of protection money.'

'How used you to pay it?'

'In cash. Used five-pound notes.'

'Handed over in the shop?'

An artful look came in the witness's eyes.

'Not in front of anyone, if that's what you're getting at.'

'I'm not getting at anything, I just want to know.'

'At first, it used to be in my office at the back of the shop. But after a time he said it was risky his being seen making too regular visits and we'd meet in a pub.'

'Is there anyone at all who can support what you say?'

'My wife.'

'Yes, but any independent witness?'

'How could there be?'

'So there aren't any?'

Mr Ferney let out a theatrical sigh. 'I can't pretend that any of this is helping me very much,' he said.

'Then I must try harder, sir,' Smeech replied in a steely tone.

The magistrate reacted as if someone had farted loudly in his court. He gazed into the middle distance with an expression of disdain.

Turning back to the witness, the defending solicitor went on, 'It's very easy to make accusations of bribery against the police, isn't it?'

'They don't seem to find it all that difficult to make false charges against innocent people.'

'Is that why you made your allegation against Sergeant Wilkley, out of spite as a sort of tit for tat?'

'What I said about him is the truth.'

'Then why that gratuitous remark about the police making false charges against innocent people?'

'Well, they do. I'm not saying all of them all the time. But everyone knows it happens. It's been proved.'

Philip Smeech, who felt he might be getting into deeper water than he would relish, removed his spectacles and gave them a polish.

'When did you first learn that Sergeant Wilkley had been suspended from duty?'

'In the Scrubs.'

'Is that when you decided to make your complaint?'

'It helped.'

'You thought you'd jump on the bandwagon?'

'I reckoned that if he was suspended, he couldn't harass me any more.'

'Are you saying that if he hadn't been suspended, you wouldn't have made your complaint?'

'I was still thinking about it.'

Ignoring Smeech, Mr Ferney turned toward prosecuting counsel. 'As I understood your opening last week, the defendant was suspended as a result of the allegation made by this witness. Is that not so?'

'No, sir. He had been suspended in respect of another matter which has nothing to do with this case.'

'Don't let's leave it wrapped in mystery,' Smeech broke in. 'The matter in respect of which he was suspended has been investigated and no further action is being taken. Had it not been for this present charge, there is no reason to think my client would not have been reinstated.' He glanced at Superintendent Evesham for a nod of confirmation, but the officer remained poker-faced.

As no one appeared to be looking in his direction, Mr Ferney tapped his desk with his pen to get attention. When this succeeded, he said, 'My court seems in danger of being turned into an "any questions" forum. Perhaps you will do me the courtesy of addressing me, Mr Smeech, when you wish to raise extraneous issues.'

'It was an issue you raised yourself, sir,' Smeech said indignantly. 'It was you who first asked about my client's suspension.'

'And *you*, if I may remind you, who intervened with an *ex cathedra* statement.'

'What the hell's that mean?' Inspector Dibben muttered to Evesham who was the nearest person to him.

Evesham shook his head as if to dislodge a fly on his cheek, as he waited to see whether the matter was going to be pursued. If Smeech had any sense, he would drop it, for the last thing Evesham could do was to give Sergeant Wilkley even a partial whitewash. It was true that the original complaint against him which had led to his suspension had come to nothing in the sense that the evidence fell short, but this was a long way from implying his reinstatement. Moreover, other matters were being looked into all the time. Sergeant Wilkley had had a long wallow in a particularly fertile midden and Ralph Tremler had been but one of its denizens.

It was at this point that Reg Atkins made his return to court. Evesham's attention was drawn to his arrival by the door he closed noisily behind him. There was something faintly triumphant about his expression and his raspberry pip was obviously giving him particular satisfaction for he was munching away like a contented cow. Evesham vaguely wondered what he had been up to to put him into such apparent good humour.

Inspector Dibben left his seat to go and whisper to the usher, who then ambled to the back of the court and began tugging at several long cords which controlled the ceiling high window. He couldn't have done more if he had wanted to steal the show and for half a minute or so he became the focus of attention as he wrestled to close the window, which he finally achieved with a clatter and a fall-out of dust on those immediately below.

'Now that that turn is finished, perhaps we can get on,' Mr Ferney said icily.

'I was asking you about the timing of your complaint, Mr Tremler,' Smeech went on. 'The fact is you waited until Sergeant Wilkley was on the ground before you decided to put the boot in yourself, that's right, isn't it?'

'Don't answer that,' the magistrate said sharply, then turning to the defending lawyer he added, 'I'm not a jury and questions wrapped in that sort of rhetoric don't impress me.'

Philip Smeech flushed angrily. He'd known difficult magistrates in his time, but Donald Ferney had succumbed to judgitis more quickly than any of them and to a particularly virulent strain at that. He really was insufferable and not only on the bench, as Smeech now knew.

'I shall adjourn for ten minutes,' Mr Ferney said and disappeared before Reg Atkins had time to lever himself from his seat.

'What's that in aid of?' Jude asked, leaning forward to speak to Miss Purton.

'I've no idea,' she replied. 'He doesn't normally take a break in the afternoon.'

'I probably shouldn't ask this, but is he as difficult out of court as in?'

'I probably shouldn't answer, but yes, he is.' Two spots of colour came suddenly to her cheeks. 'He can be a real pig,' she said in a tight tone. Then quickly smiled as if to dissipate the tension her remark had created.

'You don't surprise me,' Jude said, getting up to go and talk to Detective Superintendent Evesham, who was conversing with Inspector Dibben.

'Must make you glad you don't come to this court more often,' Dibben said with a harsh laugh.

'I can see you have quite a bit to put up with. How do you get on with him personally?' Evesham asked casually.

Inspector Dibben didn't reply for a moment. Then he said, 'I've got only a year to go for a full pension and I certainly shan't be applying for an extension. I've got a nice little pub in Dorset all lined up for me.'

'I reckon half the pubs in this country would have to close if every publican who's an ex-policeman suddenly went on strike,' Evesham said with a smile. Then in another effort to draw the inspector, he went on, 'I wonder what Ferney was like before he became a magistrate. I don't recall ever coming across him when he was in practice.'

For a time it seemed as if Dibben was not going to respond. Then he said, 'Once a shit, always a shit.'

It was at that moment that prosecuting counsel came up to Evesham's side and brought his gentle probing to an end. It had already become clear, however, that Inspector Dibben was not going to disclose his earlier encounter with Mr Ferney. An encounter which had undoubtedly had an adverse effect on his career.

While he had been sitting in court, Evesham had been having second thoughts about the sender of the two threatening letters. Surely if they were connected with the Wilkley case, that would have been made clear. As it was they were very much the product of someone working off a grievance. But would one of the court staff stoop to that sort of crude gesture? Well, he supposed Reg Atkins might, but surely not Inspector Dibben or Miss Purton. And, anyway, Inspector Dibben's cause of grievance was of such long standing that there had to be some further explanation if he was the sender. He would certainly continue making discreet enquiries, though without much hope of success. He had submitted the first letter to the lab, but their preliminary examination of the document and its envelope had failed to add anything to his knowledge. He didn't doubt that it would be the same with the second. It seemed clear that everything would hinge on the third. He was certain there would be a third and, unless the sender was a joker who was going to post one a week until he got tired, it had to declare the writer's interest.

He would have a word with his Commander when he returned to the Yard that evening about the question of protection, but Mr Ferney had made it plain that he didn't want police protection and he, Evesham, didn't think any steps were called for at the present time. But this situation could change with the receipt of the next letter.

While others were huddled in conversation inside the courtroom, Philip Smeech and his client were standing in a corner of the entrance hall. Sergeant Wilkley had lit a cigarette as soon as they had come out of court.

'It's hell sitting there not being able to smoke,' he remarked after inhaling so deeply as to suggest he wanted the effects to reach his toes.

'I'd have thought you were used to it by now. After all, you've spent a large part of your life in courts.'

'Ah, but it's different when you're anchored to the dock. Normally, one can always duck out for a quick puff. I expect that's what the poor old usher was up to, 'cept he chose the wrong moment.' He paused and glared at a reporter who was making signs at him. 'Buzz off, can't you see I'm talking to my solicitor. I'll talk to you at the end of the day.'

'I don't recommend your talking too freely to the press,' Smeech said in a disapproving tone.

'They're all right. I know most of 'em. They'll help me if they can.'

Philip Smeech made no further comment. He didn't care for his client – though there was nothing unusual about that – finding him an unattractive brash sort of person. He suspected that Sergeant Wilkley regarded him as equally uncongenial though he made every effort to hide his personal feelings when they were together. But someone whose only thoughts seemed to be on beer and blondes and racing, with all their possible combinations, and who clearly regarded anyone not sharing his tastes as peculiar was unlikely to warm to a lawyer who disliked beer, didn't smoke and had a passion for Bach. In these circumstances, Philip Smeech was flattered that Sergeant Wilkley had asked him to act on his behalf. Flattered, but not honoured.

'Ferney's a ripe bastard, isn't he?' Wilkley said, expelling a lungful of smoke at the ceiling. 'Do you think he's on our side?'

'I don't think he's on anyone's side.'

'He's got the reputation of not liking the police.' He gave his solicitor a crooked grin. 'I'm not sure where that leaves me.' A frown settled over his face. 'There are quite a few people who'll wet their pants if I get sent down. Indeed, I'll go further, they'll burst their bladders. If I go to prison, there won't just be ripples on the pond, there'll be bloody tidal waves.'

Smeech was shocked by the viciousness of his tone and even more so when he went on, 'But I don't think I shall. I think the prosecution's case could suddenly collapse. It's made up of lies, anyway.'

It was the awareness that his client's boast was not related to any skills his lawyer might deploy that caused Smeech to frown. But Wilkley didn't seem to notice as he stared across the vestibule with an expression of set determination.

'I think it's time we got back into court,' the solicitor said stiffly and walked toward the door, followed by Sergeant Wilkley who paused to grind his cigarette end into the floor.

They had barely reached their places when Reg Atkins announced Mr Ferney's return. The magistrate wore a faintly preoccupied air on resuming his seat, but he quickly shook it off as he focused his gaze on the defending solicitor.

'Have you completed your cross-examination?' he asked as though it had been going on in his absence.

'No, sir, I still have some questions to ask the witness.'

Mr Ferney let out a theatrical sigh.

'Very well,' he said, casting a long-suffering glance at the occupants of the public gallery. A glance that invited their participation in a joint ordeal. 'But please remember that the court's time is not unlimited.' Then with a malicious gleam, he added, 'If we can't finish in a reasonable time, I shall have to remand the case to a Saturday afternoon. This court has to sit on Saturdays even if it's not a very popular time for members of the legal profession.'

As both lawyers knew, Metropolitan magistrates' courts

sat every day of the year save for Sundays, Christmas Day and Good Friday, but their lists were generally arranged so that a Saturday afternoon's work did not gratuitously involve the attendance of counsel or solicitors. Mr Ferney's threat could, therefore, only be seen as punitive. It may be added that Mr Ferney and a colleague split the six days work between them, so that for the magistrate Saturday sittings were not the same penance. At the moment, Mr Ferney was the only regular magistrate at the court and the other days were taken by a relief magistrate from one of the other courts, or one of his retired brethren.

Though Jude had winced at the magistrate's words, Smeech merely greeted them with a nod of indifference. He now turned once more toward the witness who seemed wrapped in brooding melancholy.

'It's my duty to put it to you, Mr Tremler, that there isn't a word of truth in the allegation of bribery you've made against my client. What is your answer to that?'

For a second it seemed as if the witness was going to reply in one short, vulgar expletive. It could almost be seen forming on his lips. But then he checked himself and swallowed.

'What I've said is the truth,' he replied in an even tone.

'You have a number of previous convictions, don't you?'

'Why ask if you know I have?'

'Because I want to have your answer as part of your deposition.'

'Yes, I have.'

'Three of publishing obscene material?'

'If you say so.'

'Two of handling stolen property?' Tremler shrugged angrily. 'Yes or no?' Smeech pressed him.

'Yes.'

'One of forgery.'

'So-called forgery.'

36

'And one for causing grievous bodily harm?'

'That was years ago.'

'That adds up to seven convictions?'

'What do you want, congratulations on being able to count?'

'Come, come, Mr Tremler, you mustn't answer back in that way,' Mr Ferney broke in. 'Just keep calm.'

'Keep calm when my past is raked over like he's doing? It's bloody unfair. I thought justice in this country meant that once you'd done time it was behind you . . .'

'I can understand your sense of indignation, but these outbursts don't help you. Mr Smeech is entitled to question you about your record. But I'm sure the press will not go out of their way to print the details, even though reporting restrictions have been lifted at the request of the defence.' Mr Ferney glanced toward the press bench and added, 'I'm sure I can rely on the discretion of you gentlemen not to report this part of the case as it could be very unfair to the witness.'

'Is it a fact you've been to prison four times?'

'Yes,' Tremler replied, with a furious expression.

'Would you agree with me that your record isn't exactly that of a truthful and honest person?'

'What d'you mean by that?'

'That you're a person to whom lies mean nothing?'

'I've told the truth about what Sergeant Wilkley did.'

'I suggest that you've invented it.'

'Why should I invent it?'

'I suggest you invented it out of spite and malice.'

'Rubbish.'

'And that he never solicited bribes from you.'

'Huh!' The witness grunted contemptuously.

'That you've made it all up to discredit an officer who was a bit too keen on doing his job for your liking.'

'Don't make me laugh! Everyone knew he was corrupt.'

'Name some of them.'

'What?'

'Name some of the people who knew Sergeant Wilkley was corrupt, then we can check.'

'I'm not falling for that.'

'Falling for what?'

'You're just trying to trap me.'

'I'm merely following up your recent answer and inviting you to give some further details.'

'Well, I'm not doing so.'

'Because you know it isn't true?'

'It is true.'

'Is that the best you can say?'

But this time Tremler merely glowered and Mr Ferney stepped in.

'You've more than made your point, Mr Smeech; perhaps you'd like to move on to another topic, if you have one.'

The defending solicitor bent down to exchange a whispered word with Sergeant Wilkley sitting beside him. Then he said, 'I have no further questions to put to the witness.'

'I take it you don't wish to re-examine?' the magistrate said pointedly, with a quick glance at Mr Jude.

'I have just one question, sir,' Jude replied boldly.

'Very well, put your *one* question!'

'Despite your record of previous convictions, has everything you've told the court today about your dealings with Detective Sergeant Wilkley been the truth?'

'It's been the whole truth and nothing but the truth.'

'Was that all you wanted to ask?' Mr Ferney enquired frostily.

'Yes, sir.'

'I see!' He turned to the witness. 'Just listen while the clerk reads out your deposition. If there's anything incorrect in it, say so.' He looked round the court. 'And I don't want a lot of moving around or whispering while the witness's deposition is being read. It is not, as people often seem to think, like an interval in a play. It is most important that neither myself nor the witness is distracted.' He gave Miss Purton a curt nod. 'Yes, go ahead.'

In the event, the only distraction came when Reg Atkins dropped his pen which rolled across the floor and disappeared beneath the witness box. While he was retrieving it, Mr Ferney brought the proceedings to a halt and sat back in his chair with an expression of great displeasure. But the usher himself seemed unaware of the disturbance he was creating as he knelt beside the witness box and reached beneath it.

Eventually, the magistrate could stand it no longer.

'Usher, will you kindly return to your seat! The witness cannot possibly concentrate with you poking around at his feet.'

'I'm only looking for my pen, sir,' Atkins said, peering round the edge of the box.

'I'm well aware of what you're doing, but you'll have to do without it until the court adjourns. Now go back to your place. These interruptions are quite intolerable.'

Atkins scrambled to his feet and, with a wooden expression, returned to the bench on which he sat. He didn't bring himself to look at Mr Ferney, though his thoughts were not hard to read.

When Miss Purton had finished and Tremler had signed his deposition, the clerk bound him over to attend the Central Criminal Court should the magistrate commit the case for trial.

It was a few minutes before four o'clock and Mr Jude was about to call another witness when Mr Ferney said, 'I don't propose to go any further today. The defendant is remanded until next Tuesday afternoon at two o'clock. Same bail as before.'

'All this talk of how busy his court is and he breaks at least half an hour earlier than he need,' Jude said to Miss Purton after the magistrate had departed.

'He does it out of consideration for his staff,' Miss Purton replied, with a tiny glimmer of a smile. 'In fact, recording a deposition is fairly concentrated work.'

'You could have gone on for another half-hour, couldn't you?'

'I could have, but I don't mind stopping now. I still have quite a bit of office work to do before I leave.' She gave Jude another small smile. She was a pleasant woman with greying hair and spectacles, who had, however, let her figure go.

Jude had come across her on a number of occasions and thought she was competent at her job, though he gathered that administration was not her forte and that the court records had become somewhat higgledy-piggledy since she took over as acting chief clerk. Moreover, he could believe she was probably too nice a person ever to show an iron fist, even if she possessed one. He pictured her living with and supporting a widowed mother.

By coincidence, Detective Superintendent Evesham was also thinking about Miss Purton as he gathered up his papers. He had noticed that she had a copy of the *Evening Gazette* under her arm as she left court. It was hidden beneath a folder, apart from the top of the title page which protruded.

The only bit of information that the lab had been able to give him about the first threatening letter was that the letters had probably been cut from an *Evening Gazette*. The typeface and paper were identical with those used by the newspaper.

Although the *Gazette* had the smallest sales of London's

evening papers, it was still read by a considerable number of people, so that not too much could be read into Miss Purton's possession of a copy.

Nevertheless, it might be a straw in the wind. It certainly meant more than ever that it would be worth making some discreet probes into her background. Moreover, he had spent much of the afternoon observing her and had gained the impression of a woman under considerable stress.

She might appear quiet and placid, but Evesham's intuition told him otherwise. And he reckoned his intuition was as sharp as that of any female. He was prepared to bet that beneath Miss Purton's calm exterior ran some fierce cross-currents.

CHAPTER 2

Soon after Philip Smeech had returned to his office opposite the court, his telephone rang. There were two instruments on his desk; one connected to an internal switchboard via his secretary, the other a direct line to the outside world. It was this one which rang.

He lifted the receiver and said a cautious 'Hello'. Cautious because on the whole he didn't like being called on his direct line and, in fact, was very careful about giving anyone the number. Its use, as far as he was concerned, was for outgoing calls which, for one reason or another, he didn't wish to go through the office switchboard.

'Philip, it's me,' said a female voice he at once recognised.

'Hello, Rachel, I was going to call you later.'

'Have you only just got in?'

'Yes, a couple of minutes ago.'

'I tried half an hour ago and there was no reply.'

'I was in court across the road.'

'Oh, there!'

'Yes, *there*. For my sins, I spend most of my working life *there*,' he said with a mirthless laugh.

'Was it hell again?'

'Average disagreeable.'

'Poor you!'

'Poor you, too!'

'Yes, I think I probably do have the worse deal.'

'I haven't any doubt about it.'

'Am I keeping you from anything important?' she asked suddenly.

'Only work.'

'You haven't got a client waiting to see you?'

'I have one coming in about half an hour, but he's not here yet.'

'It's good just to talk to you.'

'Life that bad, is it?'

'Yes. At the moment.'

'What's happened?'

'Nothing particular's happened. It's just that I'm going through a bad spell. No special reason, other than the continuing one.'

'What can I do to cheer you up?'

'Go on talking to me, Philip.'

'I'd like to do more than that. Can't we meet again soon?'

'I'll have to find out when I can slip away.'

'Do that and let me know.'

'It'd be wonderful to have another evening out. I'm still living on memories of our last.'

'It'll be even better next time.'

'How do you know?' she asked eagerly.

'Take my word for it.'

'Happily. Do you want me to ring off?'

' "Want" isn't the right word...'

'But you feel you should get on with your work?'

'I have got some papers to read before the client comes.'

'Then I won't keep you. I already feel better for talking to you.'

'That's good. Now make sure you call me soon and let me know when we can have our date.'

'It'll be very soon, I promise you. I think he's going to be out at some dinner on Friday.'

'I'll keep the evening free.'

'Good-bye, Philip.'

'Good-bye, Rachel. Don't let him get you down!'

He replaced the receiver and left his hand resting thoughtfully on it. Yes, there was no doubt that she did have the worst deal, for being Donald Ferney's wife was far worse than practising in his court.

Detective Superintendent Evesham was a member of A10 branch at Scotland Yard, the branch which investigates complaints against police officers. When he arrived back in his office after court that afternoon, he sought out Commander Bantry who was the head of the branch.

'You're back early, Tom,' Bantry remarked.

'The magistrate adjourned early, sir.'

'Case going all right?'

'As well as can be expected, as they say of patients in hospital. Ralph Tremler stuck to his story in most of the essentials. He got a bit excited when Smeech began cross-examining him about his record.'

'That line can sometimes be counter-productive for the defence. Instead of screaming for help, the witness merely becomes bloody-minded.'

'Tremler took refuge in angry outbursts.'

'Will he impress a jury?'

'Who can tell, sir? Sometimes they seem to accept what villains say in these cases, other times they obviously don't. There are certainly weaknesses in Tremler's story, not least its timing; on the other hand, I can't see Wilkley being a very impressive witness. I just hope he'll be seen for what he is, a thoroughly corrupt copper.' Evesham paused. 'But first we've got to have him committed for trial, sir, before we start worrying about the jury.'

Commander Bantry looked at him sharply. 'Surely there's no danger of our losing him at the lower court? That'd be a complete disaster.'

'Mr Ferney's a funny sort of magistrate,' Evesham observed in ruminative tone. 'Actually, sir, he's the reason for my coming to see you. He's had another threatening letter.' He fished inside the folder he was carrying and produced the letter and its envelope which were now sealed in polythene.

Commander Bantry stared at them with a frown. 'As I recall, it's a different sort of envelope from the first: also a different postmark. The other was W.1.'

Evesham nodded. 'Correct, sir.'

'Doesn't sound very blood-curdling. Is the magistrate worried?'

'It's difficult to tell. He certainly rejected my suggestion of police protection. Or rather he passed the buck back to me.'

'Hmm, as we both know, Tom, the sort of protection we can give in such circumstances isn't even a thin blue line. Anyway, what do you propose?'

'That we let things run as they are, sir, and review the question again in the light of the third letter which I'm certain he'll get.'

'You mean "one, two, three"?'

'Yes, sir.'

'Supposing he comes to some harm before then?'

'It's because of that possibility, sir, I'm telling you about it,' Evesham said with a wisp of a smile. 'If anything did happen to him before the third letter arrives and it emerged that the police knew about the first two but did nothing to protect him . . .'

Commander Bantry held up a hand. 'No need to go on, Tom. I can picture the headlines and the questions in parliament as vividly as you can. The thing really is that the investigation of the threats isn't A10's baby at all. I know that I agreed you should make some enquiries on the side, but that was because you felt then that the threats were linked to the Wilkley case.'

'I still think it's possible, sir.'

45

'Even so, I'm not sure that the time hasn't come to pass it to C.I. They're the people to investigate it.'

'Except, sir, that there's precious little investigation to do at the moment. Also I think that the fewer number of people who know what's going on the better. At the moment, no one at Bloomsbury Magistrates' Court has been told anything. They've no idea that he's received threatening letters.'

'Are you trying to tell me, Tom, that you want to keep the enquiry?'

'Yes, sir. Because I think it will be easier for me than for a new officer from C.I.'

'I'm not entirely persuaded about that, but, if it is to be, we're certainly going to have a word with the Deputy Commissioner about the protection aspect. He can also decide whether we should go on handling the further enquiry or pass it to C.I.'

A quarter of an hour later, Bantry and Evesham found themselves in the Deputy Commissioner's room. He listened attentively while Commander Bantry outlined the situation and Superintendent Evesham added a few supplementary items of information.

He was a small bespectacled man with a genial expression and an ability to make quick decisions without agonising.

'So there are two separate questions,' he said when Bantry had finished. 'Do we try and arrange some protection for Mr Ferney? And should Evesham continue with the enquiry into the threats? I'd say "no" to the first and "yes" to the second. I agree that people don't generally warn their victims in advance and when they do, they're unlikely to go any farther. And these two letters bear all the marks of a nutcase. One can never be one hundred per cent certain, but we have to work on probabilities – and the probability is that Mr Ferney won't suffer worse than a brick through a

46

window, if that. I don't think what has happened so far merits stretching our over-stretched resources farther. Added to which, he apparently doesn't want to ride to and from court in one of our cars. He's probably safer travelling by bus, anyway. As to the other question, on the grounds of expediency if nothing else, I would prefer Tom Evesham to continue with the enquiry.'

'That's that then,' Commander Bantry said as he and Superintendent Evesham walked back to their own part of the building. 'You feed the information in, press the button and out come the answers.'

Tom Evesham felt that it would ill become him to question whether the answers were always right even though on this occasion he was satisfied.

Betsy Luke stared at the visitor, trying to make up her mind about him. Admittedly Madeleine's clientele came in all descriptions and sizes, but even so the man who faced her in the small, stuffy room seemed more unlikely than most. If he had ever been interested in sex, that time must surely belong to the past. He not only looked beyond it, but he showed none of the signs of palpitating eagerness that some of the older ones exhibited. But Betsy knew that you couldn't always go by looks.

When he had first come in, he had obviously thought she was the prostitute and she had had to explain that she was only the maid. And thank goodness for that with someone like him! But it showed he was beyond it, if he thought she, with her disfiguring facial scar, plied a successful trade.

It did occur to her that perhaps he had never had sex with a woman before and it had become a matter of now or never. That was not unknown.

The way he was standing just inside the doorway of the small, ill-lit room, she decided it was going to need dynamite

47

to move him. There was something doggedly tenacious in his attitude.

In the end she felt she had no alternative but to go and speak to Madeleine. Pointedly locking the table drawer and pocketing the key, she gave him a final appraising glance and said, 'Wait here and I'll find out if she'll see you.'

Madeleine was reclining on the settee in her bedroom. She was wearing a flimsy, black negligee and was reading the colour supplement of an old Sunday newspaper. She was an attractive woman who had taken more trouble than most in her profession to guard against the signs of wear and tear. You wouldn't find her hanging about open doorways in search of custom. The porters at some of the nearby hotels had her telephone number and, in addition, she always had a small discreetly worded card in the window of the newsagent round the corner. But the greatest boon of all was having Betsy as her maid. Betsy was able to vet the clients and find some excuse to turn away those of whom she didn't like the look. Betsy was friend and protector and well worth the commission she paid her.

'Hello, ducky,' she said as Betsy came into the room, firmly closing the door behind her. 'Someone here?'

It was six o'clock, which was often the start of the early evening business. Men on their way home after work. Then came a lull and from nine o'clock on things would usually pick up again with clients from the hotels. But today she had already had a couple between four and six. One an old regular, the second a silent but passionate Canadian.

'An old boy,' Betsy said in a puzzled tone. 'There's something funny about him.'

'Lots of old men are kinky. The older, the kinkier until they're left with only their lovely memories.'

'I don't mean kinky.'

'You don't think he's violent?' Madeleine asked sharply.

48

'Because, if so, you can push him back down the stairs double quick.'

'No, he's just persistent.'

'Like he's just come off a ship or out of prison, you mean?'

'I'm not even sure he wants sex at all,' Betsy said in a still mystified tone.

'What the hell's he come for then?'

'He insists that he must see you.'

'You're sure he's not dangerous?'

'He doesn't look it.'

'I don't think I like the sound of him.'

'He's going to be difficult to get rid of.'

'Tell him I'm out.'

'He knows you're not.'

'Tell him I'm engaged for the rest of the evening.'

'I think he'll just wait.'

'Has he got money?' Madeleine inquired abruptly.

Betsy nodded. 'I asked him to show me his wallet and I could see several fivers.'

'He showed it you without a fuss?' Madeleine sounded surprised.

'Didn't raise any objection.'

'You know what, Betsy? He sounds to me like an inquiry agent. And I don't want any of them around here. They only bring trouble. Make some excuse and get rid of him.'

Before Betsy could turn, however, the door opened and the man stood there.

'Get out of here,' Madeleine screamed at him.

'I only want to talk to you. It won't take long . . .'

'Get out! Get out!' Madeleine's screams became louder and she seized a bronze ornament from the mantelpiece and held it menacingly aloft.

The old man gave her a look of horror and quickly

vanished from the doorway. They heard him clatter down the narrow stairs and close the street door behind him.

'He was a filthy old pervert,' Madeleine observed with a harsh laugh, as she replaced the ornament.

But Betsy was frowning hard, apparently lost in thought, and didn't reply. The reason for the old man's visit had suddenly dawned on her.

She was suddenly aware that Madeleine was addressing her.

'Who were you talking to just before he came?'

Betsy blinked stupidly. 'Just before that old chap, you mean?'

'Yes.'

'Oh, er . . . it was the young man from the chemist's shop. He dropped in some things that weren't ready when I called in earlier in the day.'

'You want to watch your tongue when you're talking to him. Eric's his name, isn't it? Anyway, I don't really trust him.'

'What's wrong with him?'

'He's a bit too friendly with the police. I suspect he passes on information about people he sees around the area. If he sees any well-known face, for example.'

Betsy laughed. 'He's so short-sighted, he can hardly see across a room. Anyway, what's it matter to the police who comes visiting girls in this area?'

'The secret service keeps files on anyone who matters,' Madeleine said darkly. 'Ever since those scandals a few years back.' Her face lit up. 'But why don't we have a drink, ducky?'

They had scarcely taken a sip, however, before the front-door bell rang and Betsy went down to admit another client.

When she returned to her own small room, she sat down in the easy chair and thought about the old man again. It was Madeleine's mention of an inquiry agent that had set off her thoughts.

Just before the new client emerged from Madeleine's room, Betsy phoned home to make sure her son was safely back and had found the meal she had left for him. He was just fifteen and it wouldn't be long before he flew the nest. Meanwhile, however, nothing was too good for him. On Saturday she would buy him the padded parka on which he had set his heart. She opened her handbag and put away the twenty £10 notes she had stuffed into the pocket of her black velvet jacket when the old man suddenly arrived.

CHAPTER 3

The Ferneys lived in a pleasant house in Kew. They had been married for eighteen years, but had no children. Rachel Ferney knew that her husband resented her failure to provide him with a son.

She was four years younger than him, and at the time of their marriage he had been an ambitious and hard-working young barrister. None of his friends actually said that he had married her for her money, though it certainly hadn't been a disadvantage. Rachel was the only child of a wealthy textile manufacturer and on her parents' death in a car accident twelve years previously she had inherited £300,000.

By the time this happened their marriage was already on an arid plateau. She had tried to do her duty and please him, but it hadn't been long before she realised that she had married an overbearing and self-indulgent husband. She also suspected that, on occasions, he had been unfaithful to her.

In these circumstances, she had made a life for herself. She was on various charity committees and had become a knowledgeable and enthusiastic gardener, which, with Kew Gardens just round the corner, had proved a fulfilling choice of occupation.

Donald still expected her to play the dutiful wife on social occasions and it was in this way that she had come to meet Philip Smeech. It had been at the annual dinner of the local branch of the Law Society a few months previously. Donald Ferney had been one of the guests of honour and

Rachel had found herself sitting next to Philip Smeech who was that year's secretary.

He had told her that he was a widower, his wife having died of cancer at the age of thirty-five two years earlier. He said that, if they'd had young children, he thought he would have re-married as soon as possible, almost of convenience. But like the Ferneys, they were childless, so that even though he didn't rule out the possibility of marrying again, it was something that could happen at the right moment, should it ever come along.

Long before the meal was over, Rachel had begun to feel a rapport with her quietly-spoken and naturally sympathetic table companion. It was only later, of course, that he'd told her how he had sensed the strains in her own married life. Until then he had fondly imagined that, though an ogre in court, Donald Ferney left nothing to be desired at home.

About a fortnight after that first meeting, he had telephoned her at home and asked her out to dinner on a Saturday night. He said that he knew Donald was attending a weekend seminar at Cambridge.

Since then they had met on about half a dozen occasions when her husband was safely out of the way and the point had been reached when she felt certain that he would have suggested marriage had she been free to accept.

But of course she wasn't free and Philip was not the sort of person to put pressure on her. He had never even suggested they should spend a night together and their relationship hadn't progressed sexually beyond light kissing.

'What would Donald do if he knew we were meeting?' he had asked on the last occasion they had an evening together.

He had expected some immediate reply, but Rachel had been silent for a full minute before replying.

'One thing for sure, he wouldn't divorce me,' she said eventually with an edge of bitterness in her tone.

'He's got no grounds for divorce, anyway,' Philip had replied energetically.

'Even if he had, he wouldn't.'

'Because of your money?'

She nodded. 'I imagine we'd just go on much as now. Outwardly, that is. He'd probably remind me how forgiving and magnanimous he was.'

'Is he really capable of that amount of self-deception?'

'Easily. His sort is so full of self-esteem they can delude themselves about all their motives.'

'Doesn't he have any idea of his reputation in court?'

'He sees himself doing his duty without fear or favour and accepts that he may become disliked by a few people.'

'It's more than a few. There isn't a person at his court who has a good word to say for him.'

'I'm sure he doesn't believe it's as bad as that. But if he did, he would merely consider that he was cleansing some Augean stables. He takes good care to remain on good terms with the press and his faithful public.'

'I know. Enough to make you spit at times.'

Rachel was thinking of all this as she stood gazing out at the garden through the drawing-room french windows. January was not a gardener's month and she longed for the next few weeks to roll by and for the evenings to start drawing out.

Donald was still dressing upstairs and Velma, their foreign maid, was making breakfast to the usual accompaniment of bangs and clatters. They didn't really need her services and Rachel wouldn't mind attending to most of the chores herself with just some casual help two or three days a week, but Donald regarded Velma as a status symbol. Some status symbol, Rachel reflected as she heard a saucepan lid fall to the floor.

At a quarter to nine Donald came down to breakfast and at a quarter past, he would leave to walk to Kew Gardens station and his journey into central London.

'Oh, there you are!' he exclaimed, as he looked round the drawing-room door. 'There's a button off one of my shirts. I only discovered it was missing when I put the shirt on, so I had to get another out of the drawer. I've left the other over the chair in my dressing-room.'

'I'll sew it on,' Rachel said.

'Isn't it possible to check them when they come back from the laundry? There's nothing more irritating than putting on a shirt and then having to take it off again.'

'I always do check them. I must have missed it.'

He glanced at his watch. 'It's made me late. I hope breakfast's ready.'

His wife followed him across the hall into the breakfast-room which adjoined the kitchen. It was a rule that when they were eating, Velma would leave the kitchen and go upstairs. She was putting the last items on the table as they entered.

'Good morning, Velma,' he said with a cheerfulness that had been totally absent a few minutes earlier when speaking to his wife.

'Good morning, Mr Ferney. I hope your eggs is all right today. I have boiled just as you tell me.'

'Good girl! I'm sure they're fine.'

A few minutes later, however, he let out a long-suffering sigh. 'They're as runny as pig's swill,' he said crossly. 'Can't you teach her how to boil an egg?'

'It's probably simpler to do it myself.'

'Of course she'll never learn anything if you go round doing things yourself.'

'I'll have another word with her.'

'She's a nice willing girl. All she needs is a bit of instruction.'

'Will you be home the usual time this evening?' she asked after a pause.

'Depends what you call usual time,' he said in his stuffiest lawyer's voice.

'If you come straight from court, you're normally back by five to half past,' she replied patiently. 'Last night you weren't back until nearly seven . . .'

'I told you I was going to a meeting yesterday evening.'

'I know; I'm not complaining. What about tonight?'

'What's it matter?' he said irritably. 'I'll be in for dinner, anyway and we don't eat until eight o'clock. I might drop into my club for a rubber of bridge on my way back this evening.'

'You haven't done that for some time.'

'Precisely. That's why I might today.'

'You never seem to dine there nowadays either.'

'Food's gone off. Incidentally, I shall be out to dinner the evening after next. I've promised to dine with Giles at Gray's Inn. And I've another dinner engagement at my own Inn next week. I can't remember which evening, but I'll let you know in time.'

Rachel nodded, as she hoarded away the bits of information as if they were nuggets of refined gold. 'I'll arrange to see Sheila on Friday. I've not seen her for ages.' Sheila was an old friend of hers whom Donald cordially disliked. 'We might meet somewhere in town and eat together. I'll give her a ring later today . . .'

'All right, don't prattle on about the woman. I've never understood what you see in her. No wonder her husband left her.'

He pushed back his chair and got up.

'You've got some egg on your shirt,' Rachel remarked.

'Oh, damnation!' he exclaimed angrily and shot out of the room and back upstairs. When he came down again in his third shirt of the morning, he didn't even bother to call out good-bye, let alone look into the breakfast-room. The front door slammed and he had gone.

But she was far too excited to mind. In fact, she barely noticed.

Although there was a small yard at the rear of Blooms-bury Magistrates' Court with space for two cars, Donald Ferney never drove to work. The fact was that he disliked driving and preferred to travel by public transport, however great its frustrations and inconveniences. Being one station from the end of the line and also travelling after the main morning rush generally ensured that he obtained a seat. He liked to sit as far away from the doors as possible, so that he didn't have people standing all around him. Then he would unfold his *Times* and start reading, looking like one of those well-heeled bank managers who pop up in TV adverts. He was completely oblivious of the glances he attracted from his less immaculate fellow-travellers.

On this particular morning, however, he left the news-paper unfolded on his lap and stared unseeingly across the carriage. Though he would not have admitted it to anyone, he was worried. Extremely worried. Bravado had impelled him to reject any suggestion of police protection, but the two letters he had received had unnerved him. He had been sent a number of cranky letters in the past, but there was something different about the present missives. They didn't fall into that category, which could only mean that someone really was gunning for him. Perhaps not literally gunning, but there were other equally disagreeable possibilities. Why should anyone want to see him snuffed out? There was something casual and callous about the word itself and he gave an involuntary shiver.

At Hammersmith he changed trains and found himself glancing with suspicion at other passengers waiting on the platform. He stood well back from the edge recalling how easy it was to be pushed in front of a train. He remembered reading of a business man who suffered this fate at the hands of someone released only that day from a mental home. He, poor man, had been picked at random, but Donald Ferney would be someone's specific target. He thought he suddenly recognised a man who had been a defendant in his court and he moved well away from him until he finally had his back against a bill-board.

When he reached his final station, he emerged to find it had begun to rain and he put up his umbrella. In doing so, however, he felt he had deprived himself of a handy weapon.

But such jitters were absurd, he told himself crossly, as well as being right out of character. He really mustn't surrender to even the mildest form of paranoia.

It took him twelve minutes to walk to court. As he approached the quiet narrow lane on to which the magistrate's entrance opened, he was tempted to keep going and enter by the main door at the front of the building. But this would inevitably arouse comment, which would be worse than the minimal risk of walking eighty yards along the lane.

Clutching his umbrella more firmly, he quickened his step and half a minute later had reached the small open yard at the rear of the court. It was empty as it always was. A clerk in the general office had once sought permission to park his car there, but had been refused on Donald Ferney's instructions. He had regarded the request as an impertinence.

He side-stepped a large puddle in the yard and reached his private entrance. He had his key ready and a second later was inside the building.

As he made his way upstairs to his room, he reflected that the yard was certainly the place to ambush the magistrate if anyone had that in mind. Perhaps he ought to get one of the police officers stationed at the court to escort him just to the end of the lane when he left in the evening. After all it would be dark then.

On arrival in his room, he took off his hat and coat, after

leaving his umbrella in the corridor to drip on the brown linoleum.

As he sat down at his desk he noticed that his hands were trembling and he glared angrily at them.

Reg Atkins took his wife a cup of tea in bed every morning before leaving for court. She was an invalid and never got up until eleven o'clock. Fortunately, they had kind neighbours who were always dropping in to keep her company and who did any shopping that was required.

'Won't it be lovely when you've retired, Reg?' she said, as he put the tea on the table at the side of the bed. 'Not long to go now.'

He grunted non-committally. Living on his meagre pension was not going to be all that easy even without extravagant tastes. Moreover, he had more than a suspicion that when his wife spoke longingly of his retirement, which she did frequently, she was thinking mostly of herself. It certainly would be much nicer for her to have him around the house all day, though he viewed the prospect himself with less enthusiasm. It was not that he wasn't fond of her, but that didn't mean he wanted to become housebound in a couple of years' time.

Her gaze followed him around the room as he moved from dressing-table to hanging-cupboard and back again. Though she had never met any of them, she knew all the court officials, as if they were close neighbours, from what Reg had told her about them. He seldom came home without some anecdote of what had happened in or out of court that day. It would have hurt her considerably if she'd ever become aware how little they, in turn, knew about her, for Reg never spoke of her other than in answer to polite, if bored, questions about her health when he would simply say that she was about the same.

'You haven't told me anything about Mr Ferney recently,

Reg,' she said, as he stood brushing the fringe of hair which ran round his otherwise bald head.

'Why do you suddenly mention him?' he asked, turning his head and shooting her a suspicious look.

'I was wondering if he was less picky than he was at the beginning.'

'The only way to treat him is to ignore him,' he said as he took his black alpaca jacket off a hanger and put it on.

'Of course you used to like Mr Butterwick, didn't you?' she rambled on.

'I just get on with my job and don't take any notice of 'em,' he retorted.

'But you used to speak well of Mr Butterwick,' she persisted.

'There was nothing wrong with him.'

'They're going to miss you when you leave, Reg.'

He nodded his acceptance of the tribute.

'They don't take no trouble to train 'em these days. And all these women,' he added scornfully. 'Being an usher's a man's job.'

'Of course it is, dear,' his wife agreed loyally. 'And what about that Miss Purton as chief clerk? How's she doing?'

'She doesn't get on with Ferney.'

'You didn't think she would, did you? Thing is you've had the experience, Reg.'

'That's right and that's what counts. Experience.'

He moved across to the bed and kissed his wife on her upturned forehead. 'Nothing else you want before I go, Edith?'

'No, I'll be all right, Reg. Have a good day.'

Some hope of that, he reflected as he made his way downstairs. His pride had prevented him from telling his wife about the humiliation he had received in court at the magistrate's hands, but he was going to wipe the slate clean. He was quite determined about that.

In the hall, he put on his old army overcoat, which had been dyed a sober dark blue, and his slightly newer black homburg.

Like Mr Ferney, he also was in a thoughtful frame of mind as he travelled to court that morning. Unlike Mr Ferney, he felt not so much worried as exultant.

Miss Purton lived farther afield than either the magistrate or the usher and so her daily journey to court began earlier.

As Jude had surmised, she did live with an aged, and often difficult, mother. There was nothing physically wrong with her, apart from a bit of arthritis, but she was a naturally complaining woman who resented both that her daughter had never got married and at the same time that she left her so much on her own.

Elspeth Purton found living at home a considerable trial, but knew there was no alternative so long as her mother remained alive. For choice, she would have a small flat in town and would go to all the plays and concerts that were now merely an occasional treat.

She didn't mind not being married, but she did mind being tied to her querulous old mother. However many allowances she made for her, the fact remained she was a millstone around her daughter's neck. A thought which Elspeth Purton dutifully repelled every time it became too insistent.

She had opted for the public service as soon as she qualified as a solicitor, believing that there would be less discrimination than in private practice. The fact that Mr Ferney had laid a shadow across her career had done nothing to change her original belief, though it had filled her with considerable bitterness. It was grossly unfair that her confirmation in the appointment of chief clerk had been held up and ultimately it could affect her retirement and pension.

She still burned with indignation when she recalled how a few weeks earlier he had summoned her to his room and told her without any attempt at softening his words that he was unable to recommend her for full appointment. Since then she hadn't ceased brooding on the injustice of it and her inability to obtain a transfer to a different court had served only to rub salt into an open wound.

For several days she had taken it out on her mother by being sullen and uncommunicative and by generally displaying an abundance of ill-grace around the house. But then her conscience had rescued her and she realised that she, in turn, was behaving unfairly.

If anyone was to be the target of her feelings, it should be the magistrate and not, in this instance, her innocent mother.

As she got into her Mini and drove to the station for the fifty minutes' rail journey to London, her sense of injustice became so overpowering that it threatened to affect her driving. It wasn't the first time it had happened and it came on like a recurring fever. Today she was filled with an almost desperate recklessness, so that when she did finally reach the station car park she felt quite weak physically from the surging strength of her emotion.

Inspector Dibben had been a tough, ambitious policeman until his career in the C.I.D. had foundered and he had been transferred into the uniformed branch and subsequently posted to a backwater. For no one could pretend that being court inspector at Bloomsbury Magistrates' Court was other than a dead-end.

Mr Ferney's complaint against him had not been the first, but it had certainly, in Dibben's view, been the most unjustified. Moreover, having been largely rescued from two previous complaints about his investigating conduct by his recognised zealousness as a C.I.D. officer, it was the last one which resulted in his undoing.

He hadn't long arrived at Bloomsbury Magistrates' Court when Mr Ferney was appointed as presiding magistrate, since when their relationship had been one of chilly neutrality. That is to say, Mr Ferney addressed him only when necessary, ignoring him on social occasions such as the court Christmas party or at drinks for a retiring official. At no time had the magistrate referred to their earlier brush, nor, indeed, shown that he even recognised his court inspector. But as he took no trouble to make himself agreeable to any of the court staff, there was nothing particularly noteworthy about that.

Sitting in court day after day listening to Mr Ferney dispensing his personal brand of justice, Dibben's low view of him had been confirmed a thousand times over. How on earth did someone like him ever come to be appointed? Dibben didn't let the question bother him, for it had happened before and would happen again. In all walks of life, the four letter men clambered remorselessly up the rungs of their ladders, all too often being given helpful shoves and leg-ups by those who should have known better.

Inspector Dibben had no idea whether anyone at the court, apart from the magistrate himself, knew of their earlier encounter. He supposed it possible that one or two of the officers in the warrant and jailer's offices might know, but none of them had ever hinted at such knowledge.

Not that he cared, anyway. His retirement on full pension was not all that far off and, provided he didn't actually make off with the fines money, his position was secure. The worst that could now happen to him would be a transfer elsewhere and that would hardly be a penance.

It was with these thoughts in mind that he had been brooding about Reg Atkins' situation. He had been outraged by the magistrate's treatment of the usher and knew that, even though he had said nothing, Reg had been deeply wounded. The point was whether someone who was as much of a bastard as Mr Ferney had any idea of the effect of his public rebukes on an old and well-tried servant of the court.

It was in these circumstances that Inspector Dibben arrived at court that morning determined to have a word with the magistrate. Nothing could be lost and he had no fears for his own position. It certainly never occurred to him that the magistrate's reaction might be to double his nastiness at the expense of the unfortunate usher.

When he reached the corridor in which the magistrate's room was situated, he saw Mr Ferney's umbrella standing outside the door surrounded by a small pool of water and knew that he had arrived.

Mr Ferney's expression registered surprise when he saw who was his visitor. He had been glancing through a new set of road traffic regulations which had been placed on his desk and he kept the document in his hand as if to indicate that a lengthy interruption would be unwelcome.

'I'd like to have a word with you, sir,' Dibben said, stiffly.

'What about?' Mr Ferney's tone was not encouraging.

'About Atkins, sir?'

'Atkins the usher?'

'Yes.'

'What about him?'

Inspector Dibben bit his lip and went on awkwardly, 'I don't think you realise, sir, how much you've upset him.' The magistrate's expression became even more glacial. 'When you dressed him down in court last week, sir, and again yesterday afternoon, it was humiliating him in front of everyone. He's been here longer than any of us, sir, and, though he mayn't show it, he's a sensitive old man. You hurt him more deeply than you probably intended and I thought you ought to know, sir.'

'Is that all?' Mr Ferney inquired in a tone hung with icicles.

'Yes.'

'And may I ask what your exact role is in the matter?'

'As a senior member of the court staff, I thought I'd have a word with you.'

'Do you purport to speak for others?'

'No, sir. I've come on my own initiative.' He wasn't going to tell the magistrate he had suggested to Miss Purton that she ought to make the approach but that she had demurred.

'I suppose *you'll* be hurt if I say I think it's a gross impertinence on your part,' Mr Ferney remarked with a sneer.

'Not in the slightest, sir,' Dibben replied. His tone was unrepentant though he realised that his mission had failed.

'Well, that's how I do regard it. As far as I'm concerned, Atkins is past the job and is as inefficient as he's tiresome.'

'I'm sorry, sir, that you've taken it that way.'

'I've never had much time for people who interfere in matters that don't concern them.'

'I consider this particular matter does concern me,' Dibben retorted with a note of anger.

'Oh! In what way?'

'As a colleague.'

'A colleague, eh!'

'Yes.'

'Well, let me tell you, inspector, that how I choose to run my court is my concern and I don't need lessons from any police officer. I suppose you still bear me a grudge for reporting you on that occasion, but I was only doing my duty.'

'Is that all, sir?' Dibben asked, now pale with anger.

'As far as I'm concerned, yes.'

'Then I'd just like to say one final thing. You're even more of a bastard than I thought you were.'

He was trembling when he got outside the door and realised that his voice had been raised to a shout. He half-expected Mr Ferney to follow him out and tell him he was sacked or suspended; not that he had authority to do either. But maybe he was already getting through to the police station to which Dibben was notionally attached and demanding his removal. He had never envisaged actually losing his temper, but it was Ferney's reference to his complaint that had caught him on the raw.

'You look a bit rough this morning,' P.C. Shipling observed cheerfully when Dibben reached the jailer's office. 'Wonder if his majesty's in yet,' he went on, picking up the court register in which he had just finished recording the morning's cases.

'He is in,' Dibben said, but in such an odd tone that Shipling gave him a puzzled look.

But when the court inspector said nothing further, P.C. Shipling tucked the register under his arm and made to leave.

When he reached the magistrate's room, he found Mr Ferney staring at the wall as if he had had a sudden divine revelation.

And for once the magistrate had no critical observations to make on the list of cases ahead of him that day.

CHAPTER 4

Betsy Luke hadn't long arrived at the flat that morning when the front-door bell rang. It was a few minutes after noon and too early for it to be a client. In any event, Madeleine always slept until one o'clock and refused to see anyone before three unless it happened to be an old client and a particularly rich one at that.

Betsy supposed, as she made her way down the single flight of stairs at the foot of which lay the street door, that it was probably one of the local traders. Possibly Alf who ran a fruit stall fifty yards along the street and who knew Madeleine's passion for large Mediterranean grapes. He would often bring them to the door, hoping to make a sale.

But it was not Alf's face she saw when she peered through the spy-hole, but Detective Sergeant Wilkley's.

She opened the door and gave him an unenthusiastic look.

'Hello, Betsy,' he said with a smirk. 'Long time no see.'

'That's right,' she replied coolly, 'so what brings you here now?'

'Happened to be in the neighbourhood and thought it'd be an opportunity to drop by and say hello.'

'Well, now you've said it.'

'Oh, come on, Betsy, don't pretend you're not glad to see me. How's Madeleine by the way?'

'Asleep.'

'It's you I wanted to see anyway. Why don't you invite me in?'

'Is this an official visit?'

'I've been suspended, you know that! It's just a friendly visit.'

'You can't stay long,' she said defensively.

He gave a chuckle. 'I'm not going to frighten off any business, don't worry.'

'It's not that that bothers me,' she retorted as she turned to go back upstairs. 'It's the fact you're here at all.'

'I keep telling you, it's just a social visit. Looking up old friends, that sort of thing. I have time on my hands these days.'

They reached the small front room which was Betsy's domain and Wilkley pulled a chair out from the wall and sat down.

'You'd heard about my spot of bother, hadn't you?'

It was a silly question, for who hadn't heard of Detective Sergeant Wilkley's suspension almost as soon as it took place? In the realm in which he had worked, the bush wire was as swift and effective as any system of satellite communication.

She nodded. 'How's your case going?'

'Been following it in the papers, have you?'

'Think I saw something last week.'

'There's something in today's *Mail*. Now it's gone over to next week. Daft system, just hearing a bit and then another seven days' remand.' He glanced at the table. 'Have you got the *Mail*?'

She shook her head. In fact she had read the short account in the bus on her way to work, but was not going to tell him so. At least, not until she knew the real purpose of his call, because for sure it was not just the friendly visit he proclaimed.

'You know who's put the boot in against me, don't you?' he went on. 'It's Ralph Tremler.' He waited for her reaction, but when none was forthcoming, he repeated, 'Ralph Tremler, Betsy.'

He stared meaningly at the scar which ran down her left cheek from the lobe of her ear to the corner of her mouth.

'He's someone you'll never forget, eh, Betsy? Scarred you for life, didn't he? And all he got for it was twelve months, because *you* refused to testify. Why *wouldn't* you give evidence?'

'It certainly wasn't out of any love for him,' she said, quietly.

'Afraid of him, were you?'

' 'Course I was. We all were. He was the toughest ponce around those days.'

'So I've heard. If he thought he was being cheated by a girl, he'd shiv them before they had time to blink. You aren't the only one to carry his battle honours. There were two others he put out of business. A couple of Maltese girls fled straight home. He was never even charged with those. He'd have gone down for five years if you'd come out strong in the witness box.' He sighed. 'I can never understand people who make a statement to the police, but then get cold feet and refuse to back it up in court.'

There was a short silence and then she said, 'What've you really come about, Vic?'

'I should have thought it was obvious. Ralph Tremler.'

'What about him?'

'How much do you still hate him?'

'I've put him out of my life.'

'That doesn't answer my question,' he said, fixing her with a lopsided smile.

'I don't think about him any more.'

'But when you do?'

'It all happened years ago and I've had nothing to do with him since.'

'But you must remember him every time you look in a mirror. How's your kid by the way?'

'He's fine, but why mention him and Tremler in the same breath?'

'No offence intended.'

'If you're hinting that that lump of greasy sludge is Michael's father you can f. off now,' she said angrily.

'I'm not hinting at anything,' he said holding up his hands in mock surrender. 'I'm not prying. But at least you've answered my question. You hate Ralph Tremler's guts as much as you ever did.'

'And what if I do?' she asked belligerently.

'Cool it, Betsy, that's all. We're making progress.'

She looked at him suspiciously. 'What do you mean, making progress? I'm not interested in making any progress with you, Vic. If you think I'm going to help you just because Ralph Tremler's on the other side, you've got another think coming. I'm not interested. You must sort him out your own way.'

'Don't tell me you wouldn't seize an opportunity of getting your own back on Tremler? Even if you've had to wait ten years.'

'I'm not doing anything that might make trouble for me or Michael.'

'Who said anything about trouble, Betsy?' he said in a coaxing tone.

'Tremler spells trouble as far as I'm concerned.'

'Together we might be able to put him out of action for good.'

'I'm not interested.'

'On the other hand, *should* he come out on top, you might find him back in your hair.'

'What are you saying, Vic Wilkley?' she demanded.

'You're a bright girl, Betsy. I leave it to your imagination.'

'You can't threaten me. I've had nothing to do with

Ralph Tremler for ten years and I'm not going to get involved with him now.'

'But you'd still like to see him suffer a bit?' he urged.

'It wouldn't make me weep. Anyway, stop waltzing around the subject. What is it you have in mind?'

He gave her a knowing grin. 'I was just sounding you out. There's nothing at the moment. Depends how the case goes. I'll keep in touch with you, Betsy.' He rose from his chair. 'You see, I said to myself, if there's one person who'd like to see Ralph Tremler go down in flames it's Betsy Luke. And then next I said to myself, if there's anyone who could help you bring that about, Vic, it's that same Betsy Luke.' His gaze went round the room, paused when it came to the budgerigar in its cage on the table by the window and finally came back to Betsy. 'I knew you'd help me if you could.'

'I've not—'

'Ssh! Don't say anything you might regret!' he broke in. 'Especially in front of a witness,' he added, cocking his head in the direction of the budgerigar. 'Give Madeleine a kick in the fanny from me. I'll be in touch. I can find my own way out.' He gave her a leer. 'Should still be able to.' He paused in the doorway and turned back. 'Not having any trouble from the law these days?'

'Not since you left, Vic.'

'That's not kind, Betsy. I looked after you and Madeleine pretty well.'

'And got paid for it.'

He shook his head in mock sorrow. 'You need friends in your job. It's a rough world. And friends have to help each other.' He raised an imaginary glass to his lips. 'To Ralph Tremler's downfall.'

Betsy didn't stir as she listened to him run lightly down the stairs. He was nimble for his size, the result of having served in the navy before joining the police. He closed the street door quietly behind him.

She was so lost in thought that she didn't hear Madeleine come out of her bedroom.

'Who the hell have you been talking to all this time?' Madeleine demanded, replacing Sergeant Wilkley in the doorway.

'Vic Wilkley.'

Madeleine frowned with displeasure. 'What's he after?'

'Just dropped by for a chat,' Betsy said.

'Tea and sympathy now he's in trouble?'

'That sort of thing, yes.'

'Well, he wouldn't get either from me,' Madeleine said, turning to go back to her room. 'I think I'll have a bath. And then let's eat.'

After she had gone again, Betsy returned to her own thoughts. As she sat staring across at Archie, the budgerigar, one finger lightly traced the long scar on her cheek. Ralph Tremler had disfigured her for life as he had intended doing. She had had to give up her career as a prostitute only a few years after it had begun and, instead, become a maid. She had come to London at the age of fifteen and gone on the streets immediately. Oh, how inexperienced she had been in those days! So inexperienced and innocent as to conceive a child before her sixteenth birthday. And now she was at the ripe old age of thirty-one and all she lived for was her son, Michael. She had been a good mother and Michael had no notion what she really did for a living. She'd always told him she worked in a restaurant up West, which accounted for the hours she kept. He now knew that he was illegitimate, but not having a father around didn't seem to worry him. Happily, he was not an inquisitive boy. By the same token he accepted that his mother's scar had come about in a car accident. He had been only four at the time, anyway.

It was several minutes before Betsy roused herself. One thought was uppermost in her mind. It would take more than Vic Wilkley and the devil himself to get her to Bloomsbury Magistrates' Court. Admittedly, he hadn't got as far as suggesting the possibility, but, if he had, he would have found her adamant.

Nevertheless, his visit left her disturbed. She didn't trust him any more than she did Ralph Tremler and she wished they could both suddenly drop dead.

For all her brave words, she dreaded the prospect of Sergeant Wilkley getting in touch with her again.

Ralph Tremler had not enjoyed his previous afternoon's experience. Not one little bit. And what was worse, this was only the beginning. When the case reached the Old Bailey, he would have to go through it all over again and could expect his cross-examination to be even rougher than Smeech had made it.

It was one thing to have set the wheels in motion from a cell in Wormwood Scrubs, it was quite another to stand up months later and be publicly pilloried in Bloomsbury Magistrates' Court.

But there was no retreating now, the point of no return having been passed yesterday afternoon. Until he had actually turned up at court, he might have backed off and gone to ground, but now he was committed unless he wished to stir up an even fiercer hornet's nest. If he vanished now, it would be seen as an abject surrender. Moreover, others would swiftly move in and start carving up the small but potent empire he presided over in the basements and garrets of Soho.

He stared morosely at Reuben Huxey who was sitting on a chair against the wall. They were in Tremler's office at the rear of one of his clubs in Old Compton Street. The chair was hidden by Huxey's huge frame. It was a tubular one and capable of taking his weight. Any other sort was apt to become firewood in no time at all.

Huxey was watching his employer's face intently. He was able to lip-read and had also known Tremler long enough to have an instinctive awareness of his moods. Moreover, Tremler used a crude form of sign language to communicate his simpler instructions.

'It might be best, Ruby, if someone had a little accident,' Tremler said in a musing tone. 'I've got myself on a hook and I don't like it.'

Huxey grunted and blew the ash off the tip of his cigarette which was still in his mouth.

'The question is,' Tremler went on, 'who should have the accident?'

Huxey made two quick movements with his hands, indicating that it would be a pleasure to arrange something of the sort for Detective Sergeant Wilkley. But Tremler shook his head sorrowfully.

'That would certainly solve all our problems, Ruby, but the risks are too great. It's got to be something more subtle. And the sooner, the better. Point is I reckon Vic Wilkley's busted whatever happens. He'll never be back on this manor again. At best he'll be sent to somewhere like Croydon as a uniformed sergeant. More likely he'll get out altogether rather than that. It don't help me if he goes inside, that's why I don't want no more to do with it. I bloody don't want another afternoon like yesterday.' He raised his melancholy gaze ceilingward. 'Why'd I ever depart from a lifetime rule, never play on the same side as the coppers? I must have been crazy. But that's what the bloody nick does to you, makes you see everything different. What's more I'm bloody certain they *do* put something in the food.' He paused and Huxey waited for him to go on like an animal watchful for a cue from its keeper. 'So what we want, Ruby, is something that'll kill the case without any suspicion drifting this way. The case dies, Vic Wilkley gets shoved into the wings and the field is left clear.' He gave Huxey a small saturnine smile. 'Sighs of relief all round, eh, Ruby? So all we got to think of is how to fix it.'

Huxey let out a sequence of eager grunts and made a chopping motion which seemed to spell fatal accidents for everyone connected with the case.

Tremler took no notice and went on, 'Trouble is that almost everyone can be replaced. No good arranging a little accident for that prosecuting fellow, someone else'd turn up. Same goes for Superintendent Evesham and that cocky sidekick of his.' He sighed and gazed abstractedly at the curtained door. 'Bloody magistrate's about the only one without a substitute!' he murmured, in apparent disgust. Huxey was frowning when he looked back in his direction. 'You think about it, eh, Ruby? We've got time, but, as I've said, the sooner the better. Also I don't trust Vic Wilkley not to get up to something. As long as this case is on the boil, he's going to be getting up to tricks.' He gave a harsh laugh. 'Funny that him and me both want the same thing, if for different reasons. And to think I brought it all on my own bloody head!' He rose from his chair. 'Time you went off and did some rent collecting, Ruby,' he said with a chuckle. 'Business has to go on.' He walked across to the window and peered out into the small squalid area which was littered with empty crates and cartons. 'It's still pissing down,' he remarked, 'better take your umbrella.'

Huxey let out a strangulated grunt of mirth. His umbrella was his best friend and he never stirred without it. Keeping off the rain was only one of its uses.

CHAPTER 5

It had been an uneventful day at Bloomsbury Magistrates' Court. The list of cases had been routine and this, combined with the increasing smell of damp clothing contributed by those coming in from outside, had produced a depressing atmosphere which had settled over the court like a grey dishcloth.

Even Mr Ferney had been in subdued mood and had shown unwonted patience when Reg Atkins dropped a pile of books just behind his seat. Inspector Dibben began to think that, whatever the magistrate's immediate reaction had been, his words had had some effect. That was often the way. Someone would respond angrily to a suggestion, but would later reveal that it had not been totally ignored. Dibben was glad for the usher's sake, though he was still furious at the magistrate's words.

The day looked like finishing without any ructions and the last case had been reached. It was a matrimonial dispute which had been adjourned from the previous week to enable a social worker to make inquiries and report to the court.

Judy Nairn should never have become a social worker in the first place. She identified far too readily with her clients and was incapable of objective judgement. She held strong left-wing views which obtruded at any hint of what she regarded as reactionary comment and she left no one in any doubt that the so-called establishment was responsible for most of the country's ills and certainly for the misfortunes of the underprivileged, to whom she dedicated her energies. And if all that wasn't enough, she had an untidy and unwashed appearance as if to identify herself further with her clients.

To Mr Ferney she was anathema, but no more so than he was to her.

He was under the impression that he had already completed his day's work when Miss Purton reminded him of the adjourned matrimonial case.

'Well, where is the social worker's report?' he asked in a grating tone, as he glanced impatiently round the courtroom.

'Miss Nairn should be here, sir.'

'Well, she's not. Is there any reason why it can't go over for another week?'

At that moment, however, Judy Nairn came hurtling through a side door, she was sopping wet and her hair hung around her shoulders in dripping rat tails.

'I was told not before four o'clock,' she said as she reached the witness box and fished inside her brief-case.

'*I* never said any such thing,' Mr Ferney said in a tone of ill-suppressed annoyance.

'Someone said so,' she replied in an off-hand voice. 'Anyway, I've not been able to complete my inquiries and there'll have to be a further adjournment.'

'*Have* to be?' the magistrate echoed, as from a mountain top.

'If justice is to be done to this unfortunate woman, yes.' She looked up from her bulging brief-case and glanced at the small, anxious woman sitting in front of the dock, giving her a warm smile. 'I can't even find my notes at the moment. I was sure I had them here . . .'

'You seem to have come singularly ill-equipped to assist the court and apparently also without one word of apology,' Mr Ferney observed.

'I'm ill-equipped, sir, as you put it because I'm run off my feet. Being a social worker involves rather more than

77

issuing bus tickets to a queue of applicants. I'm unable to give nearly enough time to most of my cases, anyway. If I may say so, sir, it's courts which overburden us, often remitting cases quite unsuitable for our attention. As to an apology, I'm not quite sure what I'm expected to apologise for. Being wet in court perhaps. But whatever it is, you can have my apology for what it's worth.'

It was clear that she was on the verge of angry tears, when Mr Ferney broke in.

'I will adjourn this matter for a further week. I hope that by then you will have completed your inquiries and also be somewhat more composed. I can assure you that social workers are not the only ones who need feel hard done by. Magistrates also have much with which to put up.'

As he rose, he threw the court reporter a long-suffering glance. Reg Atkins scurried forward to open the door, calling out 'All stand' over his shoulder and a moment later Mr Ferney had gone.

'God, but that man depresses me,' Judy Nairn remarked to Inspector Dibben. 'He's so unsympathetic, so full of self-esteem, I could cheerfully hang him from his own lamp-post.' She gave Dibben a small twisted smile. 'Not that I expect you to agree, but I really don't think things will ever improve in this country without a bit of violent revolution. Peaceful social change of the right sort will take longer than it will for the north pole to melt.'

'Your client's waiting to have a word with you,' Dibben replied and moved off. Miss Purton and Reg Atkins had already left court.

Mr Ferney had decided not to ask for an escort to the station. It would require explanations he was in no mood to provide. Just before he left his room, he lifted his telephone and asked for Miss Purton's extension.

'I'm off home,' he said, 'but I thought I should let you know that I may be in a bit late tomorrow morning.'

Not long after the court building was in darkness. Everyone had left and the double outer doors had been locked and bolted for the night. Normality reigned, save, that is, for the body which lay in a grotesque heap just outside the magistrate's entrance.

CHAPTER 6

If Jeremy Burford had not had a weak bladder, it is probable that the body would not have been discovered until the next morning.

He was a student at London University and had spent the early evening drinking beer in a pub with friends. Shortly before seven o'clock, he had left to make his way home. He was a methodical young man and had allowed himself five minutes to answer nature's call when he reached Waterloo Station.

However, on this occasion he had badly misjudged his capacity – perhaps, the still persistent rain played its part – and realised that he wouldn't be able to hold out until he got to Waterloo.

Passing the end of the lane which ran at the back of Bloomsbury Magistrates' Court, he reckoned it was sufficiently dark and lonely to accommodate his emergency. He dived along it, glancing rapidly from side to side for a suitable place. Suddenly on his left there opened out a small yard and, with a heartfelt sigh, he plunged across to its farthest corner which lay in shadow.

It was as he zipped up his trousers again that he chanced to study his surroundings and become aware of something on the ground a few yards away. At first he assumed it was a bag of rubbish, then he noticed a pair of shoes protruding.

'Oh God, it's a person,' he thought. 'Must be an old vagrant sleeping rough.'

But the thought was scarcely in his mind before something told him that vagrants didn't doss down in heavy rain.

He moved cautiously across and peered at the crumpled

bundle, his eyes straining to see what lay there, his expression, if there had been anyone to note it, a mixture of horror and disbelief.

He took out his cigarette lighter and, shielding it from the rain, flicked it into life. It was then he saw the blood. It seemed to be everywhere, carried in countless rivulets. It was then, too, that he took to his heels and ran.

As he fled toward the Underground station, he decided he would call the police from one of the public telephones there. Just before he reached the station, however, he spotted a young police constable standing in a shop doorway and staring gloomily out.

Jeremy stopped in front of him panting.

'I've just found a body,' he gasped.

The constable's gaze came slowly round until it rested on Jeremy's face. Only the eyes registered suspicion. Then he bent his head in Jeremy's direction and sniffed. At that his look of suspicion deepened.

'Oh, yes?' he said. 'And whereabouts is this body?'

'I don't know the name of the street, but I can take you there,' Jeremy said urgently. 'It's about seven or eight minutes away.'

'You been drinking, sir?' the constable asked pointedly.

'Yes, but I'm not drunk. I promise you it's not a hoax or anything.'

'It'd better not be, sir. It's a criminal offence to give false information to the police and thereby waste their time.'

'I know. Section 5 (2) of the Criminal Law Act 1967,' Jeremy said with a quick self-deprecating smile. 'I'm a law student.'

The constable threw back his cape and spoke into the small two-way radio fastened to his left shoulder. Then pulling the cape back into position, he stepped out of the doorway.

'All right, take me to this body of yours,' he said in a tone that was still tinged with scepticism.

On the way he asked Jeremy for his full name and address and also where he had been drinking that evening.

'I thought you said about seven minutes,' he said, when they had been walking for that length of time.

'That was running. But it's a lane on the left about a hundred yards farther on.'

'Halfpenny Lane do you mean?'

'I don't know the name.'

'What were you doing there anyway?'

'I was looking for somewhere to have a pee.'

'Urinating in the highway's an offence, too,' the constable said with gloomy satisfaction.

'It wasn't actually in the highway,' Jeremy said wearily. 'It was an open yard abutting the highway.'

'Oh, you're one of those clever law students, are you?' the constable remarked sarcastically.

'It's left here,' Jeremy said, grateful at the prospect of imminent vindication.

When they reached the open yard, he merely pointed at the dark shape on the ground and stood back to let the officer go and see for himself. He watched him shine his torch on the body and then all around the yard. A few moments later, he was summoning help on his radio.

'Where exactly did you urinate, sir?' he asked on rejoining Jeremy. His tone had lost all its hostility.

'Over in that corner,' Jeremy said, pointing.

'And it was while you were there, you noticed the body?'

'I was just zipping up my trousers and preparing to leave.'

'You've no idea who it is?'

'I've not even seen the face.'

'You know against whose property you were urinating?' the constable asked with a faint smile.

'No idea.'

'Bloomsbury Magistrates' Court. As a law student, you'll know that's a much more serious offence than doing it in the highway.' The constable's tone was gently mocking.

'This is not Bloomsbury Magistrates' Court,' Jeremy said disbelievingly. 'I've been there. It's not even in this street.'

'This is the rear of it.'

Just then a police car turned into the lane, its headlights full on and its blue roof lamp revolving.

'P.C. 492 Ellery, sir,' the constable announced to the plain-clothes officer who jumped out as the car lurched to a halt in a large puddle, sending a deluge of water over Jeremy's legs.

'Detective Inspector Cruttenden,' the officer said, walking briskly to where the body lay in a sodden heap. With the aid of P.C. Ellery's torch he made a cursory examination of the area, before returning to the car and giving various instructions, which included the closing of Halfpenny Lane at both ends.

'This is the young person who found the body,' P.C. Ellery said, indicating Jeremy who was standing forlornly to one side. 'He's a law student,' he added significantly. Jeremy's teeth had begun to chatter and he'd have given anything to be back inside the pub with a large Scotch in his hand. 'He went into the yard, sir, to answer a call of nature,' Ellery went on.

D.I. Cruttenden frowned slightly. 'Have a pee, do you mean?'

Jeremy nodded even though the question had not been directed at him.

'When was this?'

'Not more than twenty minutes ago,' Jeremy said. 'I ran for help immediately and found this officer near the tube station. We came straight back here.'

'That's correct, sir,' Ellery said.

'Nothing been touched, has it?' D.I. Cruttenden asked, looking at each in turn.

'No, sir. Not since I've been here.'

'I certainly haven't touched anything,' Jeremy added.

'Good. Well, all we can do is await help. It won't be long arriving. Then perhaps you'd be so good as to come along to the station and make a statement. By the way where'd you live?'

'My home's in Norfolk, but I'm in digs in Ashford. I was on my way to Waterloo to get a train when this happened.'

'We'll run you to the station afterwards.'

'Thanks.' Jeremy glanced with a shiver toward the neglected body. 'Do you think you'll have trouble finding out who it is?' he asked.

'What, him over there?' Cruttenden said, following Jeremy's look. 'That's no problem. I know already. I can recognise him from the back of his head. It's Atkins, the court usher.'

CHAPTER 7

Detective Superintendent Evesham did not learn of what had happened until the next morning. No one knew of his interest and it was a small paragraph in his morning paper which gave him the news.

He was standing squashed in the train on his way to work and had the impression that most of London's two million commuters were in his own compartment when he saw it tucked away at the bottom of the page.

'Court Usher Murdered,' he read. Beneath that minor headline, it went on, 'A man, understood to be Reginald Atkins who was the usher at Bloomsbury Magistrates' Court, was found dead with head injuries near the court yesterday evening. The police are regarding the case as one of murder. Mr Atkins had served at the court for over thirty years and was due to retire shortly.'

It didn't take Evesham long on arrival at the Yard to discover that Detective Inspector Cruttenden of E Division was in charge of the enquiries and had gone to the mortuary where the autopsy was being performed.

A few minutes later Evesham was on his way there, too. By the time he arrived, it was over and he found Detective Inspector Cruttenden talking to Dr Crendover, the pathologist. Several other officers were present including one who was labelling body samples and items of the dead man's clothing like a methodical storekeeper.

Evesham stood to one side and waited until Cruttenden was free before introducing himself. In a few words, he explained his interest in the matter.

'That's the first break so far, sir,' Cruttenden remarked

when he had finished. 'From what you say it looks as if Mr Ferney was the intended victim. But what was Atkins doing there?'

'I can answer that, too,' Evesham said. 'I gather that, much to Mr Ferney's annoyance, he used to leave by the magistrate's door when it was raining. It cut his walk to the Tube station. Being stationed in the area, you probably know much more about the court than I do, Inspector, but it doesn't seem to be the happiest of places to work in.'

'None of them can stand Mr Ferney. And that woman clerk doesn't have the grip that's needed. I detest going there as you always get drawn into some feud or other.' He paused and glanced back at Reg Atkins' skinny body lying on its slab. 'Anyway, we've definitely got a murder enquiry on our hands. Not that it needed a pathologist to tell us that.'

'What cause of death does he give?'

'Comminuted fracture of the skull and severe underlying brain damage. Dr Crendover suggests we look for a piece of lead piping as the murder weapon. He thinks that more likely than a hammer.'

'If you've not found anything in the vicinity, it looks as if the murderer took it away with him.'

'Or dropped it down a drain. There's one in Halfpenny Lane not far from the scene. I've told one of my lads to search it this morning.'

'Will you be left in charge of the investigation?' Evesham asked.

'Good question, sir,' Cruttenden said with a sniff. 'As you probably know, our divisional Detective Chief Superintendent has been seconded to an outside enquiry and Detective Superintendent Smith is on sick leave at the moment . . .'

'And the chief inspectors all have their hands full.'

'That's how the story runs, sir. Moreover, once my

guvnor knows of your interest, he'll feel less inclined to detail one of his own senior officers.'

'Hold on, I'm not volunteering to run a murder enquiry. That's a bit outside A10's remit. On the other hand, I'd like to work in with whoever handles it.'

'I reckon, sir, that'll be me.'

'Fine.'

'If you're right in believing that Mr Ferney was the real target, do you think it's connected with the proceedings against Sergeant Wilkley?'

Evesham let out a heavy sigh. 'I could answer that better if I could think of a motive. In what way would killing Ferney help Sergeant Wilkley or anyone concerned in the case?'

'Ralph Tremler's a nasty piece of goods.'

'I agree, but how does it help him if the magistrate gets murdered?'

'You tell me, sir.'

'I can't, because it doesn't. Or not as far as I can see at the moment.'

'And if it wasn't connected with the Wilkley case?'

'Heaven knows there are enough people who dislike Ferney, even hate him. But there's the helluva gap between hating someone and actually killing them.' He paused. 'Fortunately! Or the murder rate would go bounding up.'

'Motive's going to be all important, sir.'

'It's the crucial issue. Until we unearth a motive, we're going to be floundering.'

There was a silence while both men pursued their own thoughts for a few moments. Then Inspector Cruttenden said, 'Of course it's always possible that poor old Atkins was the intended victim all the time.'

'But why should anyone want to kill him of all people? Have you had any time to dig into his background?'

'Lived in Balham with an invalid wife. Only daughter

87

married and living in Australia. Used to play snooker once a week at a local club and take his wife for drives into the country in an ancient Vauxhall on sunny Sunday afternoons.'

'Sounds a blameless enough existence.' Evesham rubbed the end of his nose: mortuary smells always irritated the membrane. 'If Ferney wasn't the intended victim, I'd incline to the view that Atkins was no more than a casual one.'

'With a motive like robbery, you mean?'

Evesham nodded. 'Yes.'

'Except his wallet was still in his jacket pocket with twenty quid in it.'

'I suppose the court money is locked away in a safe at night,' Evesham said in a ruminative tone. 'But what if the killer thought it was taken out each evening?' Observing D.I. Cruttenden's expression, he went on, 'I'm not suggesting it was a very professional job because it obviously wasn't. On that basis, it was a thoroughly botched job, but it'd be worth finding out if anyone might have got the impression that the money was taken out each evening. And it would have made sense to anyone with that idea that it should go out the back way.'

'I'll certainly enquire into that aspect, sir,' Cruttenden said. 'One thing *is* certain. The killer was waiting in the shadows for his victim to emerge. There was nothing casual about it in that sense.'

'Was Atkins wearing a hat?'

'A black homburg about as old as himself and about as much protection as a cobweb. We found the hat lying near the body with a great dent in it. Dr Crendover reckons there were at least four or five blows to the head, each of them of sufficient force to fracture the skull. Whoever did it had no intention his victim might survive. It was a case of overkill all right. Come and see for yourself, sir.'

It was some time since Evesham had been in a mortuary

and he rubbed his nose again vigorously as he followed Inspector Cruttenden over to the body. Reg Atkins was lying on his front and his shaven scalp had been peeled away to reveal his skull. It didn't require a professional eye to understand the nature of his injuries. It was as if a hard-boiled egg had been hurled on to a tiled floor.

'Somebody meant business, all right,' he remarked as he turned away. 'How did the invalid wife take the news?'

'An officer from Balham called round and broke it to her last night. She'd already been on to the station as he hadn't arrived home and she thought he must have been involved in an accident. I gather she was stunned by the news, as one might expect, but she didn't break down or have hysterics. That'll probably happen later. Luckily, her neighbour offered to spend the night with her.'

'Did you get in touch with any of the court staff last night?'

'One of my sergeants spoke to the jailer.'

'Jock Shipling?'

'You know him?'

'Only through the Wilkley case.'

'Yes, of course. He said he'd let the others know. I don't know who he rang. The chief clerk, I imagine. He may even have phoned Mr Ferney, though he probably left that to Miss Whatshername.'

'Purton.'

'Yes, Miss Purton.'

Evesham glanced at his watch. 'If I hurry, I might be able to catch the magistrate before he sits. It's only just after ten now. I don't doubt he'll be expecting to see me. I wonder if he will have changed his mind about protection.'

'He'll probably sit a bit later, anyway, in view of what's happened. And then they'll have a minute's silence and he'll utter some well-chosen words about their departed colleague.'

'I should think *they'll* stick in his throat,' Evesham observed, then added drily, 'Except that death brings out the hypocrite in most of us.' He buttoned up his top-coat and moved toward the door. 'Why don't we compare notes at lunchtime? I'll come along to the station.'

'Right, sir. I hope we each have something to tell.'

'It'll be good if one of us has.'

In fact it had been P.C. Shipling and not Miss Purton who had phoned Mr Ferney and told him the news. Somewhat to Shipling's surprise, Miss Purton had asked him to do so, saying that he would break it better than she would. He had the impression that she wasn't going to do it whatever he said.

The call came when the magistrate was watching the ten o'clock news and it was his wife who answered the telephone. In Mr Ferney's view, people should know better than ring up when he was watching television and such callers were liable to get short shrift.

'Thought I ought to let you know, sir,' Shipling had said immediately he heard the magistrate's voice, 'that Atkins, the usher, has been found dead outside the magistrate's entrance to the court.'

'I'm sorry to hear that,' Mr Ferney had replied in a tone devoid of sorrow or any other emotion. 'What was it, a heart attack?'

'It appears he was murdered, sir.'

'Murdered? Outside the magistrate's entrance, did you say? Oh, my God, that's terrible.'

'I don't have any further details, but I thought you'd wish to know, sir, rather than read it in the paper to-morrow.'

'Yes, thank you.'

Rachel Ferney noticed that her husband appeared nervous and mildly agitated when he returned to the room, but he said nothing and shortly afterwards went up to bed. The next morning he appeared quite composed again.

When Evesham arrived at court, he decided to go straight up to the magistrate's room and avoid, if possible, being seen by any of the staff for he realised his presence would be bound to arouse curiosity.

It was only after he had knocked on the door that he heard voices within.

'Come in,' Mr Ferney called out.

Standing in front of the magistrate's desk was Miss Purton who gave Evesham a startled look.

'Ah, Superintendent, I'm glad you're here,' the magistrate said, dismissing his chief clerk with a wave of the hand.

Miss Purton shot Evesham a puzzled and suspicious glance as she left the room.

'We were just discussing what I should say in court about our unfortunate usher's death. I told her that it wasn't to be an occasion for speeches from every quarter. That I would say something on behalf of the whole court staff and that, if there was any member of the legal profession in court, he could also say a few words, but I wasn't going to have everyone popping up to speak. It'd take the whole morning.'

'I only read of Atkins' death in the paper this morning,' Evesham said. 'I've just come from the mortuary now. He died of severe head injuries. The pathologist suggests that the murder weapon was a length of heavy metal.'

'Have the police not found the weapon?'

'No, sir. They're still searching.'

'The murderer probably took it away with him.'

'I'd think it more likely that he discarded it somewhere in the vicinity. You can't walk around with a length of blood-stained metal in your hand. Nor does it fit very conveniently into a pocket.'

Mr Ferney frowned, his normal reaction when contradicted. 'Be that as it may,' he went on, 'there can be little doubt who the intended victim was.'

'You, sir.'

'I'm glad we agree about that. Atkins' use of that door was totally unauthorised and contrary to all my instructions. But he was a stubborn old man and, I have no doubt, continued to use that way when it suited him and when he knew I'd left the building myself. Yesterday, I finished my afternoon list a bit earlier than usual and left soon after four, so whoever it was waiting to assault me mistimed it and got Atkins instead.'

Mr Ferney's choice of the word 'assault' set Evesham thinking. He imagined that the magistrate had used it euphemistically, but was it possible that assault rather than murder had been the intention? It opened up various other possibilities. Perhaps after the first blow, the assailant realised he had been recognised and went on to beat the hapless Atkins to death to silence him for all time. The number of blows and their degree of frenzy were consistent with this.

The second threatening letter had certainly said 'snuff it', but it had also said 'one, two, three'. Perhaps an assault on the magistrate had been intended as a foretaste of what was to come.

Mr Ferney's voice now broke in on his thoughts. 'I trust, Superintendent, that you are now disposed to take those threatening letters more seriously than you were.'

'I am indeed, sir. And may I take it that you're no longer averse to some form of protection?'

'You may. Mind you, I have no intention of running away, but I'm quite prepared to agree to sensible precautions. What do you propose?'

'I think an officer should escort you between your home and court morning and evening, and I'll also arrange for your local station to have some sort of surveillance kept on your home at night.'

'I trust the escort will be in plain clothes? I don't want to have a uniformed officer constantly at my elbow.'

'Certainly he'll be in plain clothes.'

'And what about when I don't go straight home of an evening? I have a number of dinner engagements coming up.'

'On second thoughts, it'll probably be sufficient if you're escorted merely from the court to the Underground station and vice versa. You're unlikely to be attacked in a crowded train.'

'What sort of arrangements were made to protect judges trying those I.R.A. cases at the Old Bailey?'

'They were a good deal more sophisticated, sir, than what is warranted in the present circumstances.'

'I think I'm entitled to the same protection,' Mr Ferney said stiffly.

'I'll speak to my superiors about it, sir,' Evesham said soothingly.

'High Court judges, stipendiary magistrates, we're all judicial officers of the realm administering the Queen's justice,' he went on in the same tone. Evesham made no comment other than a non-committal nod and Mr Ferney got up from his chair. 'I must go down to court. You'll doubtless let me know in the course of the day what arrangements you've made.'

'Yes, sir.'

He followed the magistrate out of the room. Half way down the corridor one of the clerks from the general office was nervously waiting in Reg Atkins' black gown. Mr Ferney motioned him to walk ahead. When they reached the bottom of the stairs, Evesham broke away to enter by one of the public doors. Since Miss Purton had seen him, there was no longer any point in trying to keep his visit secret and he decided he would spend a few minutes in court listening to the last respects about to be paid to its usher.

He had just taken up a position at the back when Philip Smeech came hurrying in with an anxious expression. Evesham surmised that someone had phoned him from the court and suggested he should come over and represent the legal profession.

Mr Ferney gazed round waiting for complete silence. Then folding his hands on the desk in front of him, he began speaking in a suitably solemn tone.

'Since this court adjourned yesterday afternoon, we have been abruptly deprived of the services of one of its loyal servants. I speak, of course, of Reginald Atkins who had been usher at Bloomsbury Magistrates' Court for over thirty years and who was found brutally murdered outside this very building yesterday evening. In sending our deepest sympathy to his widow and family, we must all hope that the perpetrator of this wicked deed will, in the fullness of time, be brought to justice.' Mr Ferney's voice seemed to catch as he finished, 'I ask you all to stand for one minute in respectful memory of Reginald Atkins.'

Not bad, not bad at all, reflected Evesham, considering what the magistrate really felt about the usher. As he had said to Detective Inspector Cruttenden, there was nothing like death for producing a display of ripe hypocrisy.

As soon as everyone had followed the magistrate's lead and sat down again, Philip Smeech rose quickly to his feet.

'As the member of the legal profession most frequently seen in your court, sir, I should like to endorse all you have said on behalf of the profession and to pay special tribute to the unfailing courtesy and help my colleagues and I invariably received from Mr Atkins. I learnt of his tragic death only shortly before coming here this morning and I am still shocked and stunned by the news. He was one of nature's true gentlemen and I'm sure he didn't have an enemy in the world.' Mr Ferney began to show signs of restiveness as Smeech prepared to go on. 'This is an inadequate tribute to a much loved figure, but it comes from the heart. Mr Atkins was already usher at this court when I first began practising here as a young solicitor and I shall be for ever indebted for his kindliness to me. It is a tragedy that he should have been taken from us in such a brutal manner . . .'

It was at this point that Evesham could see no reason for Philip Smeech ever to finish, as he rang the variations on his clichéed theme. But just when there seemed no end in sight, he suddenly sat down and ran a hand across his brow which was moist with perspiration.

'We will now proceed with normal court business,' Mr Ferney said quickly, before anyone could catch his eye.

Evesham made his way to the jailer's office, where P.C. Shipling was marshalling defendants like a drill sergeant a bunch of rookies.

'Hello, sir, what brings you here this morning? You're not in charge of the murder enquiry, are you?'

'No, but I have an interest in it,' Evesham replied with a smile.

'Poor old Reg!' Shipling said. 'Pity they missed their real target,' he added in a conspiratorial whisper. 'It was a tough penalty to pay for using the magistrate's entrance.'

'Who would know what time Atkins left last night?'

'I gather he stayed on giving a hand to one of the clerks and didn't leave until just before five.'

'And who's responsible for locking up?'

'I have the key to that door which leads into the side yard,' he said, nodding at a door in a corner of the office. 'Inspector Dibben is nominally responsible for securing the main entrance at the front.'

'And I suppose no one would check the magistrate's door at the rear?'

'No need to. Only he has a key at the moment.'

'At the moment?'

'Until a second magistrate is formally appointed.'

'His door's not bolted on the inside.'

Shipling shook his head. 'It's just an ordinary Yale lock. Or, rather, a special burglar-proof Yale lock.'

'But you don't need a key for getting out?'

'Alas for poor old Reg, no!' He paused as he pushed the first defendant to the head of the line-up. 'Want to know what I think, guv? You'll find your murderer tucked away in Mr Ferney's private life. I don't believe it was anyone connected with the court or any of his cases.'

'You could be right,' Evesham replied cautiously.

'I'd better get number one into court or his nibs will be creating,' Shipling remarked as he bounded off down the corridor leading to the courtroom.

P.C. Shipling's theory was one which had already occurred to Evesham. The trouble was there were so many different possibilities. A crime without a known motive was like a cross-roads without a signpost, but worse.

As he emerged into the vestibule of the court, he bumped into Philip Smeech who was standing hesitantly by the exit.

'I saw you in court just now,' Smeech said with a nervous smile. 'I can't get over what's happened. It's the most appalling tragedy. Any hopes of a quick arrest, do you think?'

'I can't answer that. I'm not the investigating officer.'

'You're not? I imagined that was why you were here this morning.'

Evesham shook his head. It was clear that the solicitor was on a fishing expedition and he had no intention of satisfying his curiosity. He wondered why Smeech had been hovering near the door. It wasn't what he would normally have expected of a busy solicitor. They were usually seen darting around like dragonflies. It now occurred to him that he had been waiting in the hope of waylaying him, or perhaps anyone who might be able to feed him some snippets of information about Atkins' death. If so, why was he so interested?

Evesham watched him run a finger round the inside of his collar and twist his neck about. He had the impression of someone suffering from more than mild physical discomfort. In fact, there was no doubt about it, Philip Smeech was a worried man.

'You look as if you're going down with a dose of flu,' Evesham said boldly. 'I'd pack work in and get off to bed.'

'No, it's just the shock of what's happened. The tragedy of that poor old man's death! It's affected me more deeply than I was prepared to admit.' Then as if some explanation was called for, he went on, 'I'd come to know Reg Atkins as an old friend with all the years I've spent at this court. Once you got to know him, he was as fine a person as anyone you could meet. It's terrible to think of a life just being snuffed out like that. If anyone had earned a happy retirement, it was he.' He gave Evesham a misty-eyed look. 'Well, I must be getting back to my office. I only came over because Miss Purton phoned me and suggested that I was the right person to speak on behalf of the legal profession.' He made to move away but then turned back. 'We meet here again next week, Mr Evesham. I don't mind telling you that I'd be much happier if Sergeant Wilkley had chosen another solicitor. Though my criminal work has always been defence, I've made a point of keeping in with the police and, quite frankly, I don't relish attacking them.'

'Are you telling me that you'll be attacking *me* when it comes to cross-examination?' Evesham enquired with interest.

'I'd like you to know that I'll only be acting on my client's instructions.'

'So you will be?'

'I shouldn't have spoken as I have, but I wanted you to know that I'm not enjoying the case.' He frowned suddenly. 'Oh, my God, is that why you're here this morning? You think there's a possible link between our case and the murder? After all, nobody can seriously believe that Reg Atkins was the intended victim.'

Shaking his head in a worried fashion, he hurried out of the main door and darted across the road to his office on the other side. Evesham stared after him. At the beginning, he had thought the solicitor was entirely in the throes of emotion. Now he was less sure. At some stage, a degree of calculation had seemed to intrude. It was as if Smeech had wished to put across an impression. If so, Evesham was left in a fog of doubt. Perhaps that had been the intention.

He looked up as he heard his name being called.

'Superintendent Evesham?'

It was one of Cruttenden's sergeants who had been taking statements from court staff about Reg Atkins' last known movements.

'Yes.'

'Detective Inspector Cruttenden would like to speak to you on the phone, sir.'

'We've found the murder weapon, sir,' Cruttenden said with a note of triumph when Evesham was on the line.

'Where was it?'

'Lying at the bottom of a drain in Halfpenny Lane, just as I suspected. Only twenty-five yards from the scene. As I surmised, it's a bit of lead piping about eighteen inches long.'

'How do you know it's the weapon?'

'It has to be. I'm sending it to the lab for immediate examination.'

'Good luck. But if it's been lying at the bottom of a drain for nearly eighteen hours, I'd expect it to have been washed fairly clean. You're unlikely to find any blood or hairs on it now.'

'That's what I'm afraid of.'

'I'd show it to the pathologist. He may be able to connect the indentations of the deceased's skull with that particular weapon.'

'I'll certainly do that, sir. How's your morning gone?'

'Rather like being in a fog and hearing curious sounds. At the moment I'm not making much sense of them.'

Inspector Cruttenden refrained from comment. No wonder he's tucked away in A10 at the Yard, he thought. Being in a fog indeed! He wouldn't last long on division with that sort of approach. In Cruttenden's book, even if you were in a fog, you didn't admit it. Not to your superiors and less still to those of junior rank.

'Marvellous how some people get promoted these days' was his final reflection as he rang off. Nice enough chap, but obviously didn't know a murder enquiry from a game of Happy Families.

CHAPTER 8

As soon as Philip Smeech reached his office, he told his secretary that he didn't wish to be disturbed. Then picking up his outside telephone he dialled the Ferneys' home number. It rang and rang and he was about to replace the receiver when Rachel answered. She sounded slightly out of breath.

'I thought you must have gone out,' he said with a mixture of reproach and relief.

'I was in the garden and wasn't sure whether it was ours or the one next door ringing. Where are you speaking from, Philip?'

'My office. Why do you ask?'

'You sounded different.'

He gave a small nervous bark of a laugh.

'Has Donald told you what happened to Atkins, his court usher?' he asked urgently.

'He told me he had been found murdered near the court.'

'Did he say anything else?'

'No. He just mentioned it as he was leaving this morning. Said I might see it in the paper.'

'Who told him?'

'Someone phoned last night. I imagine it was the police and he learnt then. He didn't say anything at the time, but he had a preoccupied look after the call and went up to bed rather suddenly. But why are you asking these questions, Philip?'

'He didn't tell you that the body was found lying just outside the magistrate's entrance at the rear of the court?'

'No.'

'Or that he was almost certainly the intended victim?'

She caught her breath. 'But, Philip, why would anyone want . . .?' The sentence trailed away.

'It's what everyone over at the court believes,' he said. 'None of them thinks Atkins was the intended victim. The magistrate was the only person supposed to use that particular door, but Atkins used to do so in wet weather as it was a short cut to the station.'

'But who would want to kill Donald?' she asked in an anxious voice.

'If the police know anything, they aren't saying. But it means we must be more careful than ever, Rachel. If they ever got to hear that we were seeing each other on the side, heaven knows what conclusion they'd draw. That's why I had to ring you right away and find out what Donald had told you.' In the same slightly feverish tone, he went on, 'Also I wanted to warn you in case the police come to see you.'

'Come to see *me*!' she echoed in a tone of alarm. 'Why should they come and see me?'

'Because you're his wife and might be expected to have useful information.'

'But that's ridiculous, Philip. You know as well as I do that Donald never tells me anything about his work.'

'I know, darling, but the police don't. And, anyway, they may decide to look into his domestic life.'

'Well, I can't help them. It'll just be a waste of their time. And surely it's obvious that if anyone wants to harm Donald, it's because of something arising out of his work. Judges often receive threats.'

'Threats are one thing. Murder is another. Judges don't get bumped off in this country however much they've outraged any of the litigants in their court. But the point is, Rachel, that, if the police do come and see you, you mustn't on any account mention my name.'

'Supposing they ask if I know you?'

'I can't see why they should.'

'But they might.'

'Tell them you've met me at one or two functions and leave it at that. But don't tell them anything that can be disproved.'

'I've only ever met you at one function.'

'Then stick to that.'

'You said one or two just now.'

'I'm sorry, I wasn't thinking. I'm so worried about what's happened . . . What might happen.'

'This doesn't mean that we can't go on meeting, does it, Philip?' she asked, after a pause. 'Because I couldn't bear that.'

'We must be terribly careful.'

'We will be. We always have been.'

'I know, but now more so than ever.'

'Donald's out tomorrow evening. He's dining at Gray's Inn with Giles Templer.'

'That'll be right up his street, dining with the Benchers.'

'So we could meet, Philip,' she went on eagerly, uninterested in discussing her husband's social predilections.

'Yes,' he said cautiously. 'But it must be somewhere we've never been before. We mustn't be seen dining too often in the same place.'

'Where shall we go then?'

'There's a new Italian restaurant in South Kensington called Albano's. I'll reserve a table for eight o'clock.'

'Make it half past seven, Philip. It'll give us half an hour longer.'

'What time will Donald get back?'

'Not before midnight. He always goes up to Giles' flat afterwards and they drink brandy.'

'What'll you tell him?'

'I've already told him. That I shall go and visit Sheila.'

'That's the friend he doesn't like, isn't it?'

'He can't stand her. So you needn't worry, Philip, he won't suspect anything this end.'

'But we must still be desperately careful.' He paused. 'See you tomorrow evening, darling.' He frowned when there was no response. 'Are you still there?'

'Yes, I was thinking,' she said slowly. 'It suddenly came to me that, if Donald really was the intended victim, he must still be in danger.'

'That was why he appeared preoccupied after getting the phone call yesterday evening.'

'Yes, how slow of me not to have thought of it before. No wonder he was a bit worried.' She gave a small mirthless laugh. 'Even Donald can have normal feelings at times. He must be worried sick. He's not a particularly brave person.'

Madeleine wandered into Betsy's room smothering a yawn. She had just got out of bed and looked a good ten years older than she was. She eyed the electric kettle on the table and then turned her gaze on Betsy who was darning a pair of socks.

'Make us a cup of tea, ducky,' she said. 'My mouth feels like the cat's tray.'

Betsy put down the sock and went over to the kettle. She lifted the lid and satisfied herself that there was sufficient water in it before switching on.

'How long's the water been in it?' Madeleine asked suspiciously.

'Not long. I had a cup myself when I came in.'

'Tea ought to be made with fresh water.'

'I suppose you'd like me to go and draw it from a well,' Betsy observed.

'Anyone coming in here and finding you darning socks would think he'd strayed into a knitting bee.'

'They're Michael's.'

'I can see they're not yours, ducky.' She put up a languid hand to cover a further yawn. 'How is your Michael?'

'Doing well.'

Madeleine shook her head in mild disbelief of Betsy's maternalism, which never ceased to astonish her.

'Wonder what he'd say if he discovered what his mother did?' she said in an idle tone.

'No reason why he ever should find out,' Betsy replied sharply.

'You really are proud of him, aren't you?'

'Of course.'

'No "of course" about it. Most girls like you would either have got rid of it as soon as they knew they were pregnant or, failing that, at least have had it adopted. But you really have been a proper little mother all the way along.'

The kettle began to steam and Betsy poured the boiling water into a mug in which she had dropped a tea bag.

'Doesn't he ever want to know who his father is?' Madeleine went on, watching her.

'He has asked.'

'And what do you tell him?'

'A ship that passed in the night.'

Madeleine giggled. 'One of those ships without a name, eh! Raiders, I call them.'

Betsy smiled, but said nothing. On the whole, she and Madeleine hit it off pretty well. She'd been with her for five years, with a six months' break two years back when Madeleine had been lured by the prospect of infinite riches to one of the Persian Gulf oil states. For someone without any illusions, she had returned remarkably disillusioned. Now, though she was quite happy to relieve her wealthy Arab clients of all she could get out of them, no power on earth would draw her farther east than Margate.

'It wasn't the same bastard who slashed you, was it?'

'Ralph Tremler?'

Madeleine nodded. 'Is he Michael's daddy?' Then observing Betsy's expression, she went on, 'O.K., ducky, we'll talk about something else. Never let it be said that Madeleine's a nosey old bag!' She put down the mug of tea which had been cupped in her hands and began turning the pages of the paper which was lying on the table. 'Isn't Bloomsbury Magistrates' Court where Vic Wilkley's appearing?' she asked suddenly.

'I believe so. Why?'

'Says here the usher's been murdered. His body was found lying just outside the court building.'

'I didn't see that.'

'It's a small bit at the bottom of the page.'

'Wonder who did it?'

'No need to look farther than Vic Wilkley, if you ask me.'

'Why should he murder the usher?'

'If there's dirty work anywhere within fifty miles of Vic, you can be sure he's had a hand in it. Next time he comes knocking on our door, you keep him out. He can make as much trouble now as ever. More, in fact.'

Madeleine finished her tea and drifted out of the room. A few moments later, Betsy heard the water running for her bath. Dropping the darned sock into her carrier bag, she got up and went over to the table where the paper lay spread out. She quickly found the item Madeleine had read aloud and bent over with an intent expression to read it for herself.

As often when she became thoughtful, she traced the scar on her cheek lightly with a fingertip. It was a gentle, caressing movement.

The Wilkleys lived on a new estate of 'luxurious modern Georgian homes' at Dulwich. Each property had been 'individually landscaped by an expert', which meant that instead of being in neat rows the houses stood in clumps like bored guests at a cocktail party. Most of the occupants were junior executives in multi-national corporations or thrusting young lawyers and accountants. Vic Wilkley was the only representative of the police. Until the cause of his downfall became public knowledge, it had been assumed by his neighbours that his wife had money, because the properties on Hillside Estate were certainly beyond the means of a detective sergeant. But now, of course, tongues wagged the other way, as they individually decided how to react to their dubious neighbour. It was made easier by the fact that the Wilkleys had never pushed themselves and the only family with which they were on really friendly terms was their immediate next door neighbours, the Fowlers. This had come about because Michele Fowler was the same age as Karen Wilkley and the two girls attended the same school.

For Vic's wife, Yvonne, his suspension followed by the court proceedings had come as a shock. But a physical rather than a moral shock and she was indignant that Vic had been singled out for victimisation. In her book, he had done nothing wrong. Everyone knew that the police were overworked and underpaid and if certain people, who were neither, liked to make them presents, why not! Machines always ran the better for being oiled and she couldn't see where the harm lay when both sides were satisfied. The trouble was that there were too many small-minded and envious people about. When at some point of the police enquiry, Detective Superintendent Evesham had visited their house and on leaving had stood for a moment surveying the fitted carpets, the 22" colour TV and the expensive Hi-Fi equipment and had then turned and said to her, 'Surely you don't think all this came out of a detective sergeant's pay, Mrs Wilkley?' she had been astonished by his question. Every job had its perks and more fool they who didn't pick them up. She had realised that it wouldn't be in Vic's interest to say so and she had kept silent, leaving Evesham to speculate whether she was plain simple or as devious as her husband.

On this particular morning, Karen had left for school and Vic was still sitting in the dining alcove with *Sporting Life* spread out in front of him and a half-drunk cup of tea at his side when his wife came downstairs from making the beds. Once that chore was completed, she felt others could wait.

'Any tea left in the pot?' she asked as she sat down at the other end of the table and reached for the unopened newspaper.

'Some, but it's cold,' he said, pushing the pot towards her without lifting his eyes from the day's racing news which he was studying.

Yvonne took off the lid and peered into the pot, as she tried to decide whether she wanted another cup sufficiently to make some more. In the end, she poured out what was left, added milk and sugar and took a sip. It was lukewarm and coated the mouth with tannin before you could even swallow it. She made a face and put her cup down.

'Give us a cigarette, Vic.'

Again without looking up, he picked up the packet beside him and tossed it down to his wife who nimbly caught it.

'Lighter too,' she said and received it the same way.

She lit her cigarette and glanced casually at the front page of the paper, finding nothing to interest her.

'Are you going out this morning?' she asked when she noticed her husband stub out his own cigarette and feel for the packet. In a moment he'd remember it was at her end of the table. 'Want these?'

This time he actually looked in her direction. 'Yep. One more before I go up and shave.'

She slid the packet down to him, followed by the lighter.

'Are you going out this morning?' she repeated.

'I haven't decided,' he said. 'I might go and have a talk with Smeech. He needs to be kept up to the mark.'

'I don't know why you went to him, Vic. You've done nothing but complain.'

'I went to him because I thought he was good and I didn't want to go to any of the regulars. Trouble with some of *them* is that everyone assumes you're guilty just because you're their client. Even so, I may have made a mistake about Smeech. I don't think he likes dirtying his hands and you can't defend successfully unless you're prepared for that.'

Yvonne sighed. 'I wish it didn't drag on so long.'

'You'll have to get used to that. Even if I'm committed for trial, it could well be a year before the case comes on at the Old Bailey.'

'It's inhuman.'

'It has its advantages, too. Gives more time for things to happen to witnesses. But I'm still hoping the case can be cracked in the magistrates' court. That's why I need to keep Smeech up to the mark.' He paused and gave her a sly smile. 'At least, we're free of money worries, even if I am only on half-pay.'

'You're sure they can never find out?'

'What? Where the money is?' She nodded. 'No, that's well out of their reach. Don't you worry about that!' He rose and stretched luxuriously, then scratched his chest.

'Ape!' she said affectionately.

After he had gone upstairs to shave and complete his dressing, she continued turning the pages of the newspaper. It was the words 'Bloomsbury Magistrates' Court' which suddenly caught her attention and she read the item about Reg Atkins' death.

By the time her husband came downstairs again, she was stacking the breakfast things in the dish-washer.

'The usher at your court's been murdered,' she said. 'Did you know?'

'Yeah, someone phoned me last night when you and Karen were at the cinema,' he replied.

'Did you know him?'

'Knew him a bit. He'd been there for about a hundred years.'

'Wonder why anyone wanted to kill him?'

Vic Wilkley shrugged. 'I've been wondering that, too.' His tone became thoughtful. 'I think I might try and find out a few details.' He went out into the hall and returned a minute later wearing a three-quarter-length fur-lined suede jacket. 'Expect me when you see me,' he said, coming across and giving his wife a quick kiss.

'What time will you be back?' she asked, giving him a faintly worried look.

'Depends. But if I'm going to be late, I'll call you.' Observing her expression he added, 'Depends who I run into.'

She watched him go out of the door and a couple of minutes later saw him backing his Jaguar out on to the road.

He disappeared for the greater part of every day and she accepted that he was busy with all the backstage preparations for his defence. She knew that, like all C.I.D. officers, he had contacts in almost every walk of life. Contacts who could help him in a showdown.

When Mr Ferney adjourned the court at one o'clock that day, Inspector Dibben slipped off his tunic and put on the tweed jacket he always kept handy. Then he left the building and made his way to a pub about half a mile away. He knew that the court building would be full of Cruttenden's men, interviewing staff and taking statements, and he wished to be right out of it.

Time would show whether the magistrate had told anyone of their angry exchange the previous day. If Mr Ferney felt himself in danger, he would undoubtedly inform the police of every grudge he knew to be borne against him and Dibben took comfort in the fact that he was in strong, if not good, company.

Everyone at court assumed that poor old Reg had been killed by mistake, but Dibben wasn't so sure. For some time he had suspected Atkins of being caught up in something dodgy. As a result, he didn't believe that the usher used the magistrate's entrance simply as a short cut when it was raining, but more probably because it enabled him to make a furtive departure. On one occasion, he had observed Atkins in the pub to which he was now making his way. He had been in earnest conversation with someone whom Dibben recognised as a notorious burglar. Something in their manner had caused him to slip away quickly before he was spotted. Reg Atkins had been at the court so long and knew all its most intimate workings so well that there were a number of ways in which he might have been able to help those in trouble with the law.

Dibben had no evidence that he had ever done so, but now, with his mysterious death, he began to wonder seriously about such a possibility. There was also the question of what he was going to tell Inspector Cruttenden's men when the time came.

He had just ordered a pint of mild and bitter and a pork pie when a voice broke in on his thoughts.

'Mind if I join you, squire?'

He turned to find Sergeant Wilkley standing behind him, with a tentative smile on his face.

'Saw you as I came in,' Wilkley went on, his smile growing in confidence. 'Seeing my solicitor this afternoon so thought I'd drop in here for a bit of sustenance first.' By this time the smile had become a grin. 'Have that pint on me, squire,' he said, as the barmaid put Dibben's drink in front of him. 'The same for me please, love,' he called out to her over the inspector's shoulder.

Dibben watched him pay for the drinks and they then edged their way from the crowded counter.

'Why don't we sit over there, squire?' Wilkley said, indicating space on a bench seat against the wall. When they were sitting down and Dibben had still not spoken a word, Wilkley lifted his glass and said, 'Cheers!' He drank thirstily and wiped his mouth with the back of his hand. 'I hope I'm not embarrassing you by my presence, squire? I suppose it's a bit of a nerve thrusting my company on you, but you've no idea what it means to be able to have a chat with a colleague. It's what I miss most of all. The comradeship.'

'Why should I be embarrassed?' Dibben asked in an awkward tone.

'Some are and some aren't. The majority go on treating one as they always did, but there are a few who just don't want to know one any more. I've seen them cross streets to avoid meeting me, as if I was carrying plague germs. I don't mind telling you, squire, that's more hurtful than anything. Because I've been charged, they assume I'm guilty. God knows I've never set myself up as whiter than white – I don't imagine there are many of us who could – but I don't like being pissed on from mountain tops by colleagues who touch their caps every time the Commissioner's name is mentioned.' He picked up his glass and drank again. 'But I could tell you weren't one of them, squire,' he said, watching Dibben carefully.

'Your solicitor was over at court this morning,' Dibben said, anxious to change the subject. Sergeant Wilkley was about the last person he'd have chosen to bump into – or, rather, be bumped into by, which was somewhat different. Their paths had crossed once or twice in the past, but only in the most casual manner and as to Wilkley's present trouble, Dibben regarded himself as entirely neutral and with no desire to alter that stance.

'I imagine you see him most days. He's your tame defender, isn't he? What's your view of him, squire? As a lawyer, I mean?'

'He's pretty good.'

'Stands up to Ferney, does he?'

'When necessary.'

'Glad to hear it. I'd been beginning to wonder if he was tough enough.' He paused for a moment and with a sudden frown went on, 'Incidentally, I saw in the paper this morning about an usher being murdered. That wouldn't be the old boy with the bald head who's constantly getting up Ferney's nose, would it?'

'Yes, Reg Atkins. That's what brought Smeech across to court this morning, to join in the tributes to Reg.'

'What was it, a mugging?'

'I don't think they've established a motive yet.'

'Who's in charge of enquiries?'

'Detective Inspector Cruttenden. He's from the local station. I also saw Superintendent Evesham at court this morning, but I don't know what his interest is. It could be just coincidence that brought him there.'

'Evesham!' Wilkley exclaimed in a startled voice. 'What the hell has your usher's death got to do with A10?'

'No idea. As I say, it was probably mere coincidence that he was in court this morning. Came along for some other reason and stayed to listen.'

But Wilkley was more than just puzzled, he was worried. 'Has Evesham got any other case at your court apart from mine?'

'No.'

'Then what was he doing there this morning?'

Dibben shrugged. 'Smeech may know. You can ask him this afternoon.'

But Wilkley's expression remained clouded. Something was happening and he was determined to find out what. Following Inspector Dibben into the pub had certainly paid off, but it was possible he could still squeeze out a bit more information.

'What's your theory about Atkins' death, squire?' he asked intently.

'I don't know as I have any theories,' Dibben said, casting his gaze round the bar as if searching for rescue. 'Maybe it *was* a mugging.'

'I can tell you don't think so.'

'All right, I don't.'

'So?'

'It's possible Atkins was tied up in something that went sour.'

Wilkley shot him a keen glance.

'Something criminal you mean?'

'I'm not saying it was so, but it's possible,' Dibben said guardedly.

'It's interesting, too. Is Cruttenden working on the same theory?'

'I can't tell you, I'm not in his confidence.'

'The newspaper report said something about the body being found outside the magistrate's entrance,' Wilkley said, as if he had just recalled the fact.

'That's right.'

'Has it occurred to anyone that Ferney was really the intended victim?'

'To everyone, I imagine,' Dibben said drily.

'Far more people must have wanted *him* out of the way.'

'Possibly.'

'Let me get you the other half, squire?' Wilkley said, jumping up and seizing Inspector Dibben's glass.

'No, thanks. One pint's enough for me at midday. Otherwise, I spend the afternoon nipping out of court for a leak.

Anyway, it's time I was getting back.' He rose quickly and giving Wilkley a brisk nod left the bar.

Wilkley walked slowly over to the bar and ordered a double Scotch. He decided there might now be better ways of spending the afternoon than paying a call on his solicitor, who wasn't expecting him in any event.

Detective Superintendent Evesham thought of criminal investigations as being like cross-country running. You slogged round a muddy course, often falling over and sometimes losing your way, but always propelled onward by a grim determination to finish. He foresaw the present enquiry made that much more difficult by the fact it was being run in tandem. Detective Inspector Cruttenden was nominally in charge, but his superiors at the Yard wanted him to keep in close touch and to continue his own line of enquiry about the threats. At some point, Evesham thought a clash was inevitable and had said so when speaking to his commander on the telephone that morning. But the message had come back to carry on.

Following this, he had sent his own message to Cruttenden saying that he might be late for their arranged meeting.

He was hovering in the corridor outside the clerks' office when Miss Purton came up from court at lunchtime. She gave him a quizzical look when she saw him waiting.

'I take it you want me, Mr Evesham?'

'If you can spare a few minutes.'

She opened the door of her own office, which was as cheerless as the waiting-room of a small country railway station, and left him to follow her in.

'What can I do for you?' she asked, eyeing him with an air of clinical detachment.

'You probably wonder why I've been around this morning?'

'Your presence certainly had not gone unnoticed.'

'Do you know anything about two threatening letters received by Mr Ferney?'

'Recently do you mean?' she asked with a sudden frown.

'One the day after the opening of the Wilkley case and the second on the day of the remand hearing this week.'

'Ah! That explains things.'

'What?'

'Why you came to see him before court this morning, for example. I assume the threatening letters are linked with the Wilkley case and now further linked with Atkins' death.'

'That's rather jumping to conclusions, Miss Purton.'

'I thought you were telling me that you'd already made the jumps.'

'But I've not landed on conclusions.'

'I see! What was the nature of the threats?'

'The first letter contained nothing specific. The second suggested that a third letter would be received and that subsequently the magistrate would snuff it.'

'And why do you connect them with the Wilkley case?'

'Because of their timing.'

'They're anonymous, of course?'

'Yes.'

'And so far your inquiries have got you . . .?'

'Nowhere.'

She turned her head away and gazed for a while, deep in thought, at the grimy wall a couple of yards outside her window. When she looked back at Evesham, she said. 'I knew nothing about the letters.'

'I asked Mr Ferney not to tell anyone.'

'Even his chief clerk?'

'Anyone. I thought it better no one should know at the beginning.'

'Was that because you suspected someone here as being responsible?'

'Anything was possible. After all, he's not the most popular of magistrates. It didn't take me long to discover that.'

'But if it was someone at the court,' she went on, with a frown, 'then it had nothing to do with the Wilkley case.'

'I agree. *If.*'

'So what is it you're asking me?'

'To tell me whether you think the threatening letters might have been sent by anyone here?'

'More likely by a disgruntled defendant.'

'I've thought of that, too. Mr Ferney mentioned one to me.'

'If you're inviting me to speculate,' she went on, fixing him with a serious look, 'I'd say that Atkins could have sent the letters. I know he felt very bitter toward Mr Ferney and resented the magistrate's treatment of him. At times, it seemed almost like a campaign of public humiliation.' She gave a small shiver. 'It was not an attractive exhibition on the magistrate's part.' She paused for a moment. 'I'm not mentioning Reg Atkins because he's no longer with us, but because these letters are the sort of childish revenge someone of his mentality might resort to. You don't expect a more educated person to descend to such a puerile level.' Observing Evesham's expression, she added emphatically, 'Well, I don't.'

'If it was Atkins, then that's an end of the letters,' he remarked. 'On the other hand it's difficult not to link them to last night's murder.'

'Assuming that Mr Ferney himself was the intended victim,' she said.

'Don't you believe that's a possibility?'

'I think it's more than that. I imagine most of us do. I'm sure it's a possibility that hasn't escaped Mr Ferney's mind,' she added in a tone which, to Evesham's ears, carried a note of secret satisfaction.

'Reverting to the letters for a moment,' he said, 'can you

suggest anyone else on the staff here who might have sent them? Anyone at all who bore Mr Ferney a grudge?'

He watched her closely as she considered the question.

'No, no one,' she said, decisively.

'Have you ever had any trouble with Mr Ferney yourself?'

She shot him a quick glance. 'You wouldn't be asking, would you, unless you already knew the answer?' she said in a challenging tone.

'So it's true that he has refused to recommend you for establishment as chief clerk?'

'Shall we say that my confirmation in the appointment has been held up?'

'On Mr Ferney's doing?'

'Yes.'

'What's your reaction to that?'

'If I may say so, Superintendent,' she said with a sudden spurt of anger, 'that's the sort of idiotic question television interviewers put to some unfortunate woman who has just seen her house burnt down with her children inside.'

'I'm sorry . . .'

'Of course, I was upset. It's unfair and I very much resent the imputation that I'm not up to the job. I wouldn't have been posted here in the first place if I hadn't been regarded as suitable. It's quite wrong that one's career can be blighted on the word of one man. It'll probably work out all right in the end, but meanwhile I'm being victimised. You've probably also heard that I've tried to get a transfer to another court where my abilities could be fairly assessed, but that's not even possible for the moment. So I'm stuck here serving a magistrate who has shown every sort of bias and prejudice and ill-will toward me.' She gave Evesham a small, twisted smile as if to cover her stirred emotions. 'Having said all that, I should also add, seeing whom I'm talking to, that if I'd ever felt driven to murder, it would not have been with a blunt instrument. Poison or guns are more ladylike ways.'

She's right, Evesham reflected. He couldn't call to mind a single woman who had cold-bloodedly bludgeoned her victim to death. Battered babies apart. It might have happened on occasions in self-defence, but hardly ever in cold blood.

'From what you've just said, Miss Purton, it's obvious that you think Mr Ferney was the intended victim.'

'I think we've all jumped to that conclusion. Isn't it the police theory, too?'

'We're still in the position of keeping every option open. The investigation has only just begun.'

'If anyone had wanted to murder poor old Reg Atkins, they'd hardly have done it on the magistrate's doorstep. And, anyway, no one outside knew of his habit of using that door.'

'I don't follow the reasoning that someone wanting to murder Atkins would have chosen somewhere else to do it, whereas anyone wanting to kill Mr Ferney would have quite naturally selected the doorstep.'

Miss Purton frowned in thought for a while, but then gave a small shrug as if the matter wasn't worth pursuing.

'It looks as if you've got a troublesome enquiry ahead,' she remarked. 'At least, it'll make a change from investigating your own kind. I don't imagine anyone enjoys being in A10.'

There was something slightly contemptuous about her tone, which nettled Evesham.

'Detective Inspector Cruttenden of E Division is actually the officer in charge of things.'

'Then what's your role?'

'I'm in it only because of possible links with the Wilkley case.'

'I see.' In a faintly waspish tone, she added, 'I suppose

detective inspectors are good enough for murdered ushers, but, if it'd been Mr Ferney, we might have expected to see the Commissioner himself in charge of enquiries.'

'The bigger the occasion, the more chiefs turn out. At the Spaghetti House siege there were more chiefs than Indians on the ground.'

It was clear from her tone, as well as from her words, that bitterness had gone deep. It was understandable. She was now obsessed with what she regarded as her unjust treatment. But it still didn't seem to amount to a sufficient motive for murder.

As Evesham walked away along the corridor, he once more reflected that, until they established a motive, they were going to be floundering. Either a motive for murdering Reg Atkins or one for murdering Mr Ferney had to be uncovered before the enquiry could get anywhere. Until then, it would be like a one-oared row-boat moving in endless circles.

If either Miss Purton or Inspector Dibben *were* guilty, it had to be for a still hidden motive. Both of them had grudges against Mr Ferney, but neither was sufficient to motivate a calculated murder.

CHAPTER 9

It was nearly two o'clock when Evesham reached Crutten-den's station and then only to learn that the D.I. had gone out in a hurry. There was a message saying that he would get in touch with Evesham later in the day, but he couldn't say when.

All he could learn was that Cruttenden had dashed off in a hurry to meet an informer who purported to have information about the murder. No one at the station knew anything more and Evesham was left to smother his irritation. What he had foreseen was already coming to pass.

An hour later his car pulled up in a road of neat, but drab, small Victorian villas in Balham. The end house in the terrace bore the date 1864 under its gable.

Number 27 was half-way along on the left-hand side. Lace curtains in the window frustrated prying eyes. Evesham opened the gate and walked up the short path to the front door, brushing against the privet hedge which surrounded the patch of garden on three sides like a stockade. It was a symbol of privacy more than an effective screen.

'Mrs Atkins?' he said to the grey-haired woman who opened the door.

'I'm Mrs Humphrey from next door,' the woman replied. 'Mrs Atkins is under the doctor with her nerves. She's had a sudden bereavement.'

Evesham nodded. 'I know. That's why I called. I'm Detective Superintendent Evesham of Scotland Yard. I'd like to talk to Mrs Atkins, if that's possible.'

'Who is it, Mrs Humphrey?' a voice called out from the front room.

'Just wait a moment and I'll go and speak to her.' Leaving Evesham on the doorstep, she disappeared inside. Returning a couple of minutes later, she said, 'Yes, she'll see you. Don't mind if I leave you? I've got a bit of shopping to do, but I'll be back in half an hour or so. I'll just show you in.'

Mrs Atkins was sitting in an upright chair with one arm resting on the table beside her. Evesham noticed a bottle of pills, a glass of water and a box of tissues all within reach.

'This is the gentleman from Scotland Yard, dear,' Mrs Humphrey announced. 'I'll leave you two to it then. You'll be all right until I get back, won't you, dear?'

Mrs Atkins nodded uncertainly and dabbed at her mouth with a tissue.

'I didn't catch your name,' she said after Mrs Humphrey had bustled out.

'Evesham. Like the town near the Cotswolds.'

'I'm glad it's a Scotland Yard case,' she said. 'Reg deserved that. It shows what they thought of him.'

Evesham decided this was unanswerable and that it was wiser not even to attempt a reply.

'I'm afraid your husband's death must have come as a terrible shock to you, Mrs Atkins, and you have my deepest sympathy.'

'Everyone liked my Reg. He was a wonderful husband and I don't know how I shall manage without him.' Evesham waited for tears to come but she remained dry-eyed. 'I'm semi-invalid, you know,' she went on. 'I can't do much and Reg was so good to me.'

Evesham nodded sympathetically. 'I gather you have kind neighbours who can do things for you, but is there anyone to come and look after you until everything is sorted out?'

'My only daughter lives in Australia. She's been out there twenty years. Married with five children. Someone's phoned and told her about her father. Of course she hasn't the money to come back and I suppose she can't very well leave her family anyway.'

'Perhaps when this is all over, you could make a trip out there.'

'I could never go in an aeroplane,' she said emphatically. 'I can't travel at all on account of my nerves. Reg used to take me for drives in the car, but we were never out more than two hours, otherwise I'd get one of my turns.'

'Do you have no relatives in this country?'

'My cousin lives at Southport. She's a widow and she's coming tomorrow. She'll stay with me for a while.'

'Good. That sounds like a sensible arrangement.'

'We don't get on too well,' Mrs Atkins said in a tone of quiet satisfaction. 'She's one of those domineering types. Thinks she knows best all the time. But she means to be kind in her own way, I suppose.'

It had not taken Evesham long to decide that Mrs Atkins was one of those women who enjoyed ill-health. He suspected that there was nothing much wrong with her nerves, but that she liked being the centre of sympathetic attention.

After a short silence, during which she sipped some water, he said, 'I'd like to ask you some questions about your husband. You see, at the moment we have no idea who killed him and you may be able to help us.'

'One must always try and help Scotland Yard,' she replied with a vigorous tone, as if she were being summoned to patriotic duty.

It seemed a curious reply and he wondered for a moment whether her mind was all right.

'So far as you're aware, Mrs Atkins, did your husband have any enemies?' he asked, hoping that a direct question might produce a straight answer.

'He couldn't stand that Mr Ferney,' she said without hesitation. 'He liked Mr Butterwick; you know, the one before Mr Ferney. But Mr Ferney was always picking on Reg, trying to humble him like.'

'Your husband told you this, did he?'

'He didn't tell me half of it, I'm sure of that. But I always knew from his manner when the magistrate had been at him. He didn't have to tell me, I could see.'

'You're not suggesting that Mr Ferney had anything to do with your husband's death, are you, Mrs Atkins?'

'I've never met him. I only know what Reg said about him. And what he didn't say about him,' she nodded meaningly.

'Your husband may have regarded the magistrate as an enemy – and with justification – but I doubt if Mr Ferney regarded him as one. Not sufficient to murder him, that is.'

'I can only say what I know,' she said with a note of obstinacy.

'Anyway, apart from Mr Ferney, did your husband have any other enemies?' Evesham enquired, deciding that discretion prevented his telling Mrs Atkins that her husband wasn't alone in his dislike and that to try and convince her that the converse didn't necessarily follow would be a waste of time.

She shook her head. 'Everyone liked my Reg. They were going to miss him when he retired. He'd been there that long, he could run the court on his own. There was nothing he didn't know about it. He mayn't have talked a lot, but he missed nothing, did my Reg. He had experience. As he used to say to me, "It's experience what counts, Edith." People don't worry about it so much these days, do they? Nowadays it's all a question of smart talk. But Reg never had time for that sort of thing. He just got on with his job and left others to do the same.'

In the pause that followed, Evesham asked, 'Had he mentioned Mr Ferney recently?'

Her mouth quivered and she wiped away a sudden tear.

'Only yesterday morning before he left, I asked him whether Mr Ferney was being less picky. He'd just brought me up a cup of tea and was getting ready to go.'

' "Picky", did you say?'

'You know, picky, picking on Reg.'

'Ah, yes; and what did he say?'

'He just said that he ignored him. But I knew he was still persecuting him. I could tell. It was just that Reg didn't want to worry me.'

'Did your husband have many friends in the neighbourhood?' Evesham asked, going off on a new tack.

'He had his mates at the billiards club. He and Mr Humphrey used to go there every Friday evening.'

'What about other evenings?'

'We'd just watch the telly. Reg wasn't one for going to pubs, though he liked a drink now and then.'

'Did he gamble at all?'

'Horses, do you mean?'

'And dogs.'

'He used to have a bet on the Derby and the St Leger.'

'But he wasn't a regular betting man?'

'No, he used to say it was a mug's game.'

Eveham smiled. 'I'm sure he was right.' After a pause, he went on, 'Used he always to come home at the same time?'

Mrs Atkins' expression clouded over as she nervously screwed up the tissue she was holding.

'It's funny you should ask that,' she said, at length. 'He always used to. He'd be back in the house five o'clock regular. Never after half past. If he was held up at court, he'd call me and say when he'd be home. But just this last week, he's been late a couple of times. One evening last week, I think it was Thursday, he wasn't back until after seven and then just two days ago, it was nearer half past seven before he came in.'

'Did you ask him what had made him late?'

'Yes. The first time he said there'd been a breakdown on the line. And on Tuesday, he told me he'd run into an old friend and gone to have a drink with him.'

'Did you believe him?'

'He did smell a bit of beer. But then he often had half a pint with his sandwiches at lunchtime.'

'Would you have expected him to phone you and explain?'

'Well, I would have and I told him to. I'd begun to get worried.'

And last night, he didn't phone or come home at all, Evesham reflected.

'What did he say when you reproached him?'

'He said he was sorry, but the phone in the pub had been out of order and he hadn't realised how late it was.'

'Did he seem his normal self when he came in?'

'That's the other thing. He seemed sort of excited. As though he was bursting with news.'

'But he didn't tell you anything?'

'No.'

'Was he like that both times he came in late or only the second time?'

'Only on Tuesday.'

'Did he mention the name of the friend with whom he'd been drinking?'

'Jack, he told me.'

'Do you know of any Jack who's a friend of his?'

'No. He said I'd never met him. It must have been some-one from his court days. I've never met any of his court friends, you see.'

'But he's often talked to you about them?'

'Yes. I feel I know some of them as if I saw them every day.'

'But you'd never previously heard of Jack?'

'No. I can't say that I had. But I was so relieved to have him safely home, I didn't give it a thought.'

It was shortly after this that Mrs Humphrey returned.

'How are you, dear, all right?' she asked, as she bustled into the room. 'Had a good talk with the gentleman?' she went on, without waiting for a reply. 'I expect you're both ready for a cup of tea. I'll pop the kettle on.'

'That's very kind, but I must be on my way,' Evesham said, getting quickly to his feet. He turned to Mrs Atkins. 'I hope I haven't exhausted you. It's been most helpful talking to you and I shall be in touch with you again. Meanwhile, here's my number if you want to phone me about anything.'

'There is just one thing,' Mrs Humphrey said. 'The funeral. She's been worrying about the funeral.'

'As soon as the coroner releases the body, the arrangements can be made.'

'And when will he do that?'

'It depends on various factors. I can't see that there should be any hold-up, but it's not my decision.'

'Can it be a long time?'

'It can be, yes. But I hope it won't be. I know how distressing it can be for a widow not to be able to bury her deceased husband.' He gave Mrs Atkins a quick glance, but she appeared not to be listening.

'Who'll let me know about his pension?' she asked abruptly. 'I'll be entitled to something, shan't I? Reg would want that.'

'I'm sure someone'll be in touch with you about that quite soon,' Evesham said in a hopeful tone.

For all her nerves, Mrs Atkins' feet were firmly planted in reality.

As he drove back into central London, he decided that his visit had been distinctly worthwhile. At last, there was something to work on.

Why had Reg Atkins arrived home late two nights in the past week? His explanations seemed facile and Evesham was not disposed to accept them.

Sudden breaks in a person's normal routine were always worth investigating. And never more so than when that person was shortly afterwards murdered.

When Detective Superintendent Evesham got back to the Yard, he put through a call to Cruttenden's station, only to learn that the D.I. was still out and no one could say when he would be back.

About five o'clock, however, Evesham's phone rang and he was told that Detective Inspector Cruttenden wished to speak to him.

It always irked him when he had to wait for the originator of a call to come on the line. And the fact that it was Inspector Cruttenden who now had him holding a silent receiver to his ear did nothing to soothe him.

'Hello, sir,' Cruttenden's voice suddenly cracked into life. 'Sorry I had to cancel middle day, but I had a break and couldn't hang around. Hope you haven't been trying to get me the whole afternoon. I only got back a short time ago.'

'What was the break?' Evesham asked, deciding to ignore the imputation that he had nothing better to do than wait on detective inspectors. It was clear that Cruttenden was feeling pleased with himself. Evesham felt that he could almost read his thoughts. While detective superintendents of A10 sat around in their offices, he, Cruttenden, went out and got results.

'Detective Sergeant Smith of West End Central phoned me this morning to say he had an informer who'd come up with something, so I thought I'd better go and find out what it was all about. Sergeant Smith keeps a special eye on Soho and his informer works at one of the strip clubs in the area.

'He was in a pub in Wardour Street last night when he

bumped into someone who knows Reuben Huxey. He can do the sign language so can talk to him. Anyway, this bloke who knows Huxey had been with him earlier that day and told Sergeant Smith that Huxey had talked about putting a magistrate out of action. Sergeant Smith's informer didn't think much about it at the time, but when he read in the newspaper this morning about Atkins being murdered outside the magistrate's entrance at Bloomsbury Court, he got in touch immediately with Sergeant Smith who phoned me.'

'And what's the upshot?' Evesham enquired in a determinedly unexcited tone.

'Huxey has disappeared,' Cruttenden said with a note of triumph. 'And if that isn't significant, I don't know what the word means.'

'What do you mean, he's disappeared?'

'Just that. Hasn't been seen round any of his usual haunts since last night.'

'Have you spoken to Ralph Tremler?'

'This afternoon. He didn't want to talk. Said you were the only officer he'd speak to. But I told him we were working on the matter together. Not that he knows any more than I'd already found out. Says he last saw Huxey in the early afternoon of yesterday. Huxey normally comes in around half past eleven in the morning, but today he's not turned up. I had the impression, sir, that Tremler was worried and could have said more if he'd wanted. He did say, however, that he was sure Huxey had nothing to do with the murder. But as far as I'm concerned the hunt it on and I shan't be satisfied until I've found Huxey and shaken the truth out of him.'

'I can't see what benefit either Atkins' or the magistrate's death would bring Tremler,' Evesham said in a dampening tone. I say Tremler because if Huxey *was* responsible, it's inconceivable he was acting on his own initiative.'

'We'll know more about that, sir, when we find him,' Cruttenden said robustly.

'Have you examined his room? He lives over a Chinese restaurant in Rupert Street.'

'Yes, I've searched it. Bed appeared to have been slept in last night, but no one's seen him this morning. At least that's what they say. Trouble about the whole of that area is the way they all clam up when you begin asking questions. It's all see no evil, hear no evil, speak no evil dished out with helpless shrugs and bland smiles.'

'Huxey's about as inconspicuous as the dome of St Paul's. It shouldn't be too difficult to find him.'

'Provided he shows his face. My bet is someone's hiding him.'

'Probably.'

'That's all I have to report at the moment, sir. It's been a hectic day. And it's by no means over yet.' His tone seemed to imply that it was a wonder to have found Evesham still in his office at five o'clock and that he would doubtless be off home hours before a lowly D.I. on division could get away. 'By the way, did you find out anything at court this morning, sir?' he enquired as an apparent after-thought.

'Only that they're all convinced that Ferney was the real target. Incidentally, I've made arrangements for him to be protected. Surveillance of his home at night and an officer to escort him to and from the station at both ends of his journey. It's not perfect, but what is in that line? Even the top Kremlin boys could be bumped off if anyone was single-minded enough and was prepared to lose his own life in the endeavour.'

He decided not to relate the details of his interview with Miss Purton nor of his visit to Mrs Atkins. There would be time for that later. He would like to make a few further enquiries of his own first.

One he put in hand as soon as Cruttenden had rung off. He had to wait only ten minutes before his contact at London Transport Board headquarters called back to say that there had definitely not been any breakdowns on the Northern Line to Balham on the evening Reg Atkins had given this as his excuse for being home late. For good measure, he had added, there hadn't been any that week at all.

Evesham was not surprised by the information, which merely confirmed his suspicions. He was now even more sure that the mysterious drinking companion, Jack, was equally a convenient figment of Reg's mind, though he would be less easy to disprove than the delinquent train.

As he sat staring thoughtfully across his office, he had no doubt that his own break was considerably more significant than Detective Inspector Cruttenden's.

Just what had Reg Atkins been up to those two evenings that required him to lie about his lateness home?

CHAPTER 10

By the time the weekend came, however, Evesham felt that he had got little farther forward.

All efforts to fill in Atkins' missing hours on the two evenings in question had failed. On each occasion he had left Bloomsbury Magistrates' Court between half past four and a quarter past five – though even this was conjecture – and had arrived home in Balham some two to two and a half hours later. Normally, his door-to-door journey took thirty minutes or just over.

If he had spent one evening drinking with Jack, Evesham was no nearer being able to put flesh and blood on that elusive figure. Moreover, enquiries at more than two dozen pubs within a mile radius of the court had proved equally fruitless.

Detective Inspector Cruttenden was still looking for Reuben Huxey and Evesham had himself gone to visit Tremler about his aide's disappearance.

'I don't know what's happened to him, honest, I don't,' Tremler had said with an earnest attempt at conveying conviction. 'He does this sometimes. Disappears like. But he always turns up again.'

'But why should he disappear of a sudden?' Evesham had pressed.

'Search me! Who knows what goes on in that basin head of his? He's not an ordinary bloke like you and me.'

'I certainly endorse that.'

'Well, there you are! That explains it.'

'But I thought you understood him.'

'Understood Ruby? Sometimes I think I'm crazy to

employ him. It's like keeping King Kong as a pet. You never know when he won't turn and snap your bones like dry twigs.'

'But you must have some idea where he hides on these occasions.'

'Honest I don't,' Tremler said, managing to look more melancholy than ever.

'But don't you ask him where he's been and why he went, when he comes back?'

'No point. He'd tell me if he wanted me to know. Look, Mr Evesham, I know it's hard for you to understand, but Ruby's not like an ordinary employee. You can't just push him around. He lives in a world of his own and you have to respect it. But one thing I'm sure of, he had nothing to do with this bloke's death. Why, he didn't even know him. Why'd he want to get rid of some old court usher?'

'He might do if he thought it'd help you.'

'Help me?' Tremler had sounded genuinely surprised. 'How's it help me?'

'Supposing he intended killing the magistrate? After all, as you say, he didn't know the usher. He just waited outside the magistrate's door and assumed it was the magistrate coming out. Later he learnt that he'd killed the wrong person.'

Tremler had stared at Evesham with just a bit too much wide-eyed innocence.

'But how's it help me if the magistrate gets bumped off? I'm on your side. I'm helping the police. Remember?' He shook his head slowly in sorrowful reproach. 'It'd be much more likely to help that bastard, Wilkley. Anyway, I've given my evidence, so what'd be the point of removing the magistrate now? Tell me that!'

And on this challenging note, their meeting had come to an end. Despite Tremler's protestations, Evesham still had the feeling that he knew more about Huxey's disappearance than he was prepared to say. He even had a strong suspicion that Tremler not only knew where Huxey was hiding, but had provided the hiding-place.

Detective Inspector Cruttenden spent a large part of Saturday in his office reading through again the statements which had been taken in the hope that some clue might suddenly jump out at him. Or, at least, that he might spot some inconsistency that hadn't been noticed earlier. Murder investigations often reached the stage where the only thing left to do was re-read all the statements a second, third and fourth time, tabulating, cross-referencing and analysing as you went. Solid routine, with a touch of luck added, had solved more cases than any other method.

He and Detective Superintendent Evesham had had one meeting and a number of telephone discussions during the past three days and Cruttenden had let out a sigh of relief when the Yard superintendent had not, as he had feared, moved in to the murder headquarters he had set up at the station.

He didn't attach the same significance to Reg Atkins' missing hours as Evesham did. His own theory was that the usher probably had a lady-friend tucked away somewhere whom he used to visit for home comforts. After all he had an invalid wife who was presumably unable to provide him with any.

Evesham had agreed that this possibility couldn't be excluded solely on the grounds of Reg Atkins' age. After all, older men than he still took an interest in sex. But, if Cruttenden was right, he wondered why there had been only the two occasions and both of them within the last week of his life.

Cruttenden had brushed this doubt aside by saying that possibly he had only met her recently or had taken to visiting her at a different time.

'Perhaps he used to go in the lunch adjournment before.

I'm told that's a popular time for the over-fifties,' he had added in a dismissive tone. But Evesham had remained unpersuaded.

As Cruttenden sat poring over the statements that Saturday morning, he pictured Evesham on a golf course or perhaps out shopping with his wife or taking the dog for a walk. It would have surprised him considerably to know that the A10 superintendent was also at work in his office and, in fact, remained there until after four o'clock, by which hour Cruttenden was at home watching a needle soccer match on television.

Someone who normally did play golf every Saturday, when he wasn't sitting in court, and often on Sundays as well, was Donald Ferney. He was a member of a club about twenty miles out of London and usually set off immediately after breakfast, not returning before six o'clock.

However, it came as no great surprise to his wife when he announced that he wouldn't be playing this particular Saturday. What happened was that when he retired to the drawing-room after breakfast to read his *Times*, she had asked whether he wasn't going and he'd replied tersely that no he wasn't.

He had been obliged to explain, albeit grudgingly, the loitering police constable who was now to be seen in the vicinity of their front gate for much of the day and the police patrol car which, from time to time, pulled up outside on a routine visit.

He said that it was on account of some silly threats he had been receiving and which *he* didn't think for one moment were connected with the usher's death. He clearly didn't wish to talk about either matter and he reacted testily to questions.

Rachel could tell, however, that he was worried. More worried, in fact, than she had ever known him. Moreover, it was worry mixed with fear. Having him at home all day in his present frame of mind was a prospect she relished less than usual.

Indeed, his presence provided her with a worry of her own, for Philip Smeech often phoned her on Saturday mornings, confidently expecting Donald to be out of the house.

Thankful that, at least, there wasn't an extension in the drawing-room, she closed the door firmly behind her, leaving her husband concealed behind his newspaper.

It was about a quarter of an hour later that the phone rang and, even though she was upstairs where there was an extension, she came hurrying down to the hall where she could keep an eye on the drawing-room door.

'Hello, darling, it's me,' Philip said as soon as she had lifted the receiver and hissed a wary hello. 'You sound funny. Are you all right?'

'He hasn't gone to golf today,' she said in a whispered rush.

'You mean he's in the house?'

'Yes.'

'Oh! Would it be better if I called you later?'

'Yes. No, I'll call you when I can.'

'Is it because of the murder?'

'Yes. But I mustn't stop now.'

'All right,' he said in an understanding whisper. 'I'll be in all day.'

As she rang off, the drawing-room door opened and her husband stood there like a suspicious deity.

'Who were you talking to?' he asked, with a frown.

Rachel gulped and felt herself blushing. 'It was Baynards ringing to say that the book I'd ordered had now come in.'

'What book?'

'A new one on gardening I saw advertised in one of the

Sunday papers,' she said with as much aplomb as she could manage.

'Why do you talk to them in whispers?' he asked in the same suspicious tone.

'It probably sounded like that because I have a bit of a sore throat this morning.'

'You've not mentioned a sore throat before.'

'Because I can tell you've got worries of your own and, anyway, it's not that bad.'

'If it's not that bad, why should it add to my worries?'

'Donald, I refuse to stand in the hall and be cross-examined in that hectoring tone,' she said angrily.

He shrugged. 'Well, at least, it seems to have brought your voice back,' he retorted as he turned back into the room.

Feeling flustered, angry and not a little anxious, she returned upstairs. Donald had obviously been suspicious or he would not have come to the door. He obviously didn't believe her story about the book, which was the first thing that came into her head, Baynards having phoned with the information the previous afternoon. She would not put it beyond him, however, to ring them and check on what she had said. Well, she would deal with that if it arose. If he wanted to establish a *casus belli*, she was prepared for battle. It was as a result of her dinner with Philip Smeech the previous evening that she had come to realise she was ready for a breach. She had suddenly realised that Donald needed *her* rather than the other way around. Certainly financially and for reasons of image. She had, nevertheless, decided that she still wouldn't force the pace, but if he wanted to, she was ready for him.

Well, at least, she didn't need to be housebound. She would go out and do some shopping. And call Philip from a public box.

She was putting on her coat when the bedroom telephone

extension let out a mild tinkle and she knew, at once, that Donald was on the phone downstairs.

He would know if she lifted the receiver to listen in, so she waited a few minutes before opening the bedroom door and descending.

'Hold on a moment, would you?' he said quickly, before covering the mouthpiece and watching her come down.

As she passed him in the hall, she said. 'You can tell Baynards that I'll pick the book up in the next hour.'

It was a good curtain line and she had the satisfaction of seeing his head jerk back as if she had caught him a blow on the point of the chin.

She found it difficult to credit how uncaring she felt about her husband's fate. It was a measure of the extent to which her love had withered and was now seemingly dead.

Betsy Luke and Madeleine had always squabbled about whether Betsy should have Saturdays off as of right.

'I'm not a government office,' Madeleine was fond of saying. 'If I have to work every day, why shouldn't you?'

'Because I have Michael to think of,' Betsy would reply and Madeleine would realise she was up against a brick wall.

In the end an uneasy compromise had been reached. Provided Michael was occupied in some school activity on a Saturday, which was quite often the case, Betsy was prepared to come in to the flat. But otherwise not. Madeleine continued to wheedle and moan, but it all fell on a deaf ear. Both of them were aware that good maids were not easy to come by. It was a service that required tact, shrewdness and a readiness to cope with physical violence if one of the clients suddenly exhibited such a propensity.

When Madeleine was really annoyed, she would rail against Betsy and say it was a wonder she didn't frighten off clients with her unsightly scar. The odds were that she did frighten some away, she would add vindictively. But

Betsy would merely look at her as if she was a child in a tantrum and Madeleine would eventually burst into tears and say she was sorry.

On this particular Saturday, however, Betsy had departed from the normal arrangement. She was staying at home even though Michael was going to be out all day on a sponsored cross-country run down in Kent. He had left at nine o'clock to pick up the school bus which was taking them. She had watched him stride off along the road, his sports bag slung over his shoulder. He looked so confident about life that it sometimes worried her. By all the rules, he should have been a nervy boy with a mass of hang-ups, but he was the very reverse of this. Betsy realised that some of the credit was hers, but it didn't prevent her feeling immensely grateful that he was rapidly growing to be a fine young man. She prayed that it would last, at the same time aware that he was now of an age when young people's lives can undergo sudden earthquakes.

She had fought hard to keep him and provide him with a loving background and now she was having her reward.

When Madeleine had enquired the previous day whether she would be appearing on Saturday, she had said a firm 'no'. Madeleine had assumed it was because Michael would be at home and Betsy had no intention of disabusing her and setting off another train of recrimination.

The truth was that she needed time to herself to think and she couldn't do that sitting in Madeleine's stuffy front room with a budgerigar making its silly little noises and with the interruptions of phone calls and men at the front door. And if there weren't phone calls and men arriving, then it would be Madeleine restless and wanting to talk.

Since his visit a few days before, she knew it was only a matter of time before Vic Wilkley popped up in her life again. His assumption that she would help him destroy Ralph Tremler had had a disquieting effect on her. She had told him bluntly that she had no wish to become involved, but Vic Wilkley wasn't easily put off when he had made up his mind on a certain course and he certainly was not above applying pressure to get his way.

And it was this that was worrying her. The nature of the pressure he could bring to bear. Not that she herself wasn't used to applying pressure when it pleased her to do so, she reflected with a small grim smile. But it was very different to be at the receiving end.

After Michael's departure, she went into the kitchen. She normally spent most of Sunday morning cooking for the week ahead, but, with the house empty, it was an ideal opportunity to get on with it. But more than that she always found cooking enabled her to think and sort out problems while her hands were busy pastry and cake making.

She had just put a number of items into the oven and decided to make some meringues as a treat for Michael, when her thoughts, which had been going round in circles, suddenly crystallised. She was missing one piece of information to enable her to reach a decision. Suspicion was not enough. She required confirmation.

She had no idea how to set about it, but, at least, she now knew what she had to do. She would finish her cooking and spend the afternoon on her quest.

The risks involved never occurred to her at the time. In any event, it was not so much the dangers that might follow success, as the use she made of it.

She never lacked resource and by the time the meringues were baked, she had decided on her course of action.

Detective Sergeant Wilkley spent the Saturday morning polishing his car and noting which neighbours furtively crossed to the farther side of the road to avoid having to speak to him. It didn't offend him in the least. In fact, it amused him and he took a perverse pleasure in calling out a greeting and watching them pretend not to have heard.

After an early lunch he would go and watch Charlton play a home match. That was preferable to spending a domestic afternoon with Yvonne and Karen.

He felt that the week had ended better than it had begun. Much better. If he had played the right cards – and he didn't have any doubt about it – then he might expect to see results quite soon. And they could hardly be other than satisfactory.

Miss Purton had opted to sit on Saturday with a relief magistrate and take Monday off. That would give her two days less with Mr Ferney.

It was extraordinary how different the atmosphere was when he wasn't there. The relief magistrate had recently retired from another court and was only too pleased to be summoned back for further duty. He was not only glad of the money, but delighted to have something to do. This meant that he was very much on his best behaviour as he knew that any adverse comments would destroy his future chances of being invited back. He was particularly gracious to Miss Purton, thanking her for her help and complimenting her on the efficient running of the court.

When they reached the end of the morning list, he consulted her about the length of the adjournment and asked if she would mind making it a bit longer than the usual as it would give him an opportunity of going off to his club for lunch. Saturday afternoons were normally light anyway, and on this particular one there was work for not much more than an hour, so it was agreed they wouldn't resume until half past two.

It didn't matter to Miss Purton, though she noticed P.C. Shipling's faintly mutinous look. She had forgotten that he liked to get home as early as possible on Saturdays. Well, half an hour was not going to make that much difference to him, she decided, though it would be prudent not to say so.

By the time she reached her room at the far end of the corridor from the magistrate's, their visiting magistrate had already left the building.

She invariably brought sandwiches with her, preferring them to the cellophane-encased ones from the café along the road. She usually also brought a flask of coffee, which she found more drinkable than Elsie's brew.

She had just finished her lunch and was neatly refolding the paper in which she wrapped her sandwiches when she made one of those spur of the moment decisions. She would go and have a look round the magistrate's room. She had no particular purpose in mind other than a general snoop. It was not a pastime she approved of; on the other hand she reasoned that there were occasions when it was perfectly justifiable – even proper – to resort to it.

It seemed that the thought had barely entered her head when she was tiptoeing along the corridor. She paused outside the magistrate's room and listened. But all she could hear were her own heartbeats. In one quick movement she entered and closed the door swiftly behind her.

Then as if drawn by a magnet, she tiptoed across to the desk and began trying the drawers. There were three on each side and the two top ones were locked. The next two down each contained stationery. Official court stationery in the left-hand one and die-stamped paper with his home address in the other. The two bottom drawers were deeper. In one was a pile of his old court notebooks, in the other a curious miscellany of clothing. A woollen scarf, a funny little corduroy cap, a pair of black slipper shoes and a box of shoe-cleaning material.

With a small grimace of disappointment she closed the drawer. She remembered having once had to turn out the drawers of a male colleague who had died suddenly and finding an even odder assortment of articles, including a pair of carpet slippers, a tin of golden syrup and an expensive leatherbound copy of Keats. She had learnt later that he used to buy early editions of books and then be afraid to take them home and face his wife's remonstrances.

She turned her attention again to the two top drawers, giving them hefty tugs in case they were jammed rather than locked, but they still resisted and it was clear that they were locked. A quick search for the keys was equally fruitless and it was with a feeling of deflation that she accepted her snooping had failed to reveal anything of real interest.

What had she hoped to find out? she asked herself as she returned to her own room. She didn't really know. But definitely something rather more telling against Mr Ferney than a scarf, a cap and a spare pair of shoes.

The thought of the two locked drawers nagged her throughout the afternoon.

When Philip Smeech's phone rang in the middle of the morning and he lifted the receiver to hear the imperious bleeps that indicated a call from a public box, his first impulse was to replace it immediately. Calls from public boxes invariably meant a client in trouble and that was the last thing he wanted on this Saturday morning. It also annoyed him that certain of his clients had no compunction about phoning him at home.

While he wavered, he heard the coin being inserted and a second later Rachel's agitated voice.

'Hello . . . hello . . . is that you, Philip?'

'Yes. But what's happened?' he asked in a tone to match her own.

'Nothing's happened. I said I'd call you back as soon as I could.'

'But you sound all worried.'

'I always get flustered by these coin boxes. You either

drop your money on the floor or can't get it into the slot; you get cut off; I hate them. And worst of all, they smell like a thousand unemptied ashtrays.'

'Thank goodness, that's all,' he said with a note of relief. 'I thought for one moment, something awful had happened. Where are you speaking from?'

'I'm in Richmond. Maybe it has.'

'Maybe what has?'

'Maybe something awful *has* happened. I think Donald suspects.'

'What, us?' he said in a horrified voice.

'I think he was listening when you phoned me. He wanted to know who I was talking to.'

'You didn't tell him?'

'Of course I didn't. I said it was Baynards Bookshop calling to say that a book I'd ordered was in.'

'But you don't think he believed that?'

'I'm quite certain he didn't. He was on the phone himself just as I was leaving the house and I'm pretty sure he was ringing Baynards to check on what I'd told him.'

'That's awful, Rachel,' he said in a leaden tone.

'He may suspect me of something or other, but he can't possibly associate you with it.'

'I pray not,' he replied grimly. 'But once he starts sniffing around, heaven knows where the scent will lead him.'

'Then I'll lay a false trail.'

'For heaven's sake, don't do anything hasty, darling! We must think very carefully before we make any rash moves.'

'Oh, you and your lawyer's caution,' she said with a small brittle laugh.

'It's a pity more people don't show it in situations like this.'

'All right, but what line shall I take if Donald taxes me when I get home?'

'You must hold him off.'

'What does that mean?'

'Don't admit anything. Refuse to discuss his suspicions.' There was a silence at the other end of the line and he hurried on, 'I know it's easy for me to talk, darling, but it's vital that Donald doesn't discover the truth. Suspicion is one thing, but if he finds out what's really happening we're done for.'

'You mean, you're done for.'

'All right, I'm done for.'

'But I don't understand why, Philip. After all, I'm sure I'm not the first magistrate's wife to have deceived her husband. Or to have gone off with a member of his profession. He'd still go on being a magistrate and you'd still be a solicitor. You don't get struck off for that sort of thing. It's not like a doctor and his patient. I can't see why you're so worried. What can Donald do to you?'

'It's all a question of timing, Rachel,' he said in a heavily patient tone. 'I agree with all you say, but it's vital that we control events and not have them run away from us.' He paused. 'Are you listening, darling?'

'I'm listening.'

'Don't you see that if Donald found out about us now, he'd immediately connect it with the threats he has received and with the plot to murder him. He'd be bound to and, what's more, he would inform the police. He'd tell them he had evidence that his wife was carrying on with the solicitor who had the busiest practice in his court and they had better turn their enquiries in that direction. He would be handing them what they're still looking for, what they need more than anything else.'

'I'm not with you,' she said with a note of obstinacy in her voice.

'A *motive*, that's what. Who would like to see Donald removed more than the man who covets his wife?'

'Don't sound so biblical.'

'Doesn't matter how I sound, darling, it's the truth. So now do you see why Donald simply mustn't find out about us?'

'Yes. But I'm only able to face him if I know you're supporting me.'

'Of course I'll be supporting you. Every sinew and blood vessel will be working overtime. I love you, Rachel.'

'Say that again.'

'I love you.'

'Now, I'd better go. There are three angry-looking people outside waiting to use the phone. I'll call you again as soon as I can to tell you what happens when I get back. Wish me luck.'

'I wish you more than that, my darling.'

Philip Smeech put down the receiver and mopped his brow, then wiped his spectacles which had become misted over.

He felt completely wrung out. Pray God that he had regained control of events – albeit the Almighty was unlikely to respond favourably to such a prayer in the circumstances.

CHAPTER 11

Mr Ferney recognised the envelope as soon as he entered his room on Monday morning. It had been placed on top of his other mail which consisted only of obvious circulars and a book catalogue. The clerk who had put the letters on his desk clearly reasoned that one bearing a first-class stamp took precedence over the rest.

Even though it was a different envelope from the previous two, he knew what it would contain. It was the name and address printed with a fine ball-point pen which gave it away.

For several seconds, he stood staring at it as if half-expecting it to show sudden signs of life.

It bore a W.C. postmark, the same as before, and showed Saturday's date stamp. All this his eye took in before he slit the envelope open and extracted the sheet of paper inside. He unfolded it with care and saw the familiar pattern of cut-out letters and words. This time it read:

'There won't be any mistakes next time, Ferney.'

He was still staring at it, when there was a knock on his door and P.C. Shipling came in bearing the court register.

He quickly shuffled the letter beneath his newspaper, while Shipling gave him a curious look.

'Oh, of course, the register,' he said. Just like he was coming out of a dream, Shipling later remarked to a colleague in the jailer's office.

He glanced down the list of the morning's cases with a preoccupied air and as soon as Shipling had departed, put through a call to Scotland Yard.

Half an hour later Evesham was standing in the now

familiar room. In the court below there was a subdued buzz of speculation when it become known that Mr Ferney was in the building, but would be delayed in taking his seat on the bench.

'Posted in West Central on Saturday morning,' Evesham said thoughtfully. 'In time for the first collection from the mark. That means posted before nine o'clock. I'll have to check, but there are two Saturday collections from most boxes in the central London area. One around nine and a final one about one o'clock.'

'Personally, I find the message itself of greater moment than the postmark,' Mr Ferney observed acidly. 'It makes it unmistakably clear that I *was* the intended victim when Atkins was killed. Obviously some madman is out to get me.'

'You think it's a madman?' Evesham asked, giving the magistrate an intent look.

'Who else would want to kill me?'

'Incidentally, I've checked on that defendant you mentioned to me last week, sir, and I'm satisfied he had nothing to do with it. Neither he nor the woman who passes as his wife.' He paused and went on in a thoughtful tone. 'I don't know whether it's significant or not, but the first letter arrived the day after you'd begun hearing the Wilkley case, the second arrived on the actual day of a hearing and now this one comes the day before the next hearing.'

'Yes, you're right, Superintendent,' Mr Ferney said with an unwonted note of respect in his tone. 'That could be significant.'

'Though I can't think in what way,' Evesham added quickly.

'But it's something to work on?'

'Yes.' He realised he had only agreed because Mr Ferney seemed to expect it. The magistrate had clearly been unnerved by receipt of the latest missive and was in a mood to clutch at straws.

'I've not specifically asked you this before,' Evesham went on, 'but . . .' He paused as he tried to think of the most tactful way of putting his question. 'But could these threats be linked to something in your non-official life?' He had been about to say 'private', but 'non-official' sounded slightly less offensive.

Mr Ferney frowned. 'You mean my life away from court?'

'Yes.'

'Implying that I have a skeleton in my cupboard?'

'I'm implying nothing of the sort, sir. If there is a skeleton, it might be in someone else's cupboard.'

'But I'd obviously have to know about it.'

'I suppose you would.'

'There's no supposing at all. If it's in someone else's cupboard, the implication would be that I'm blackmailing them and they're going to kill me.'

'Put like that, sir, I agree that it sounds preposterous.'

'Thank you, at least, for that admission. However, let me assure you that I'm not a blackmailer.'

Evesham took a step toward the door. There seemed nothing further to be achieved by talking to the magistrate.

'I'll send this latest missive over to the lab, sir, but I doubt whether it'll reveal anything more than the previous two. Whoever's the sender is taking good care that he can't be traced. No finger prints and the envelope's addressed in a disguised hand.'

He became aware that Mr Ferney wasn't listening to him, but was staring hard into space. Evesham paused a moment, then turned to leave the room. He had reached the door when the magistrate suddenly spoke.

'There is one thing I now feel I ought to tell you,' he said in a curiously weary tone. 'It's not something I find easy to talk about. It concerns my marriage. My wife and I have had a somewhat strained relationship for some years, but just recently I've become suspicious that there's another man. I can't tell you who, but I'm sure I'm not wrong. There've been numerous little telltale signs. She's been pressing me for precise details of when I'm going to be out. There've been small displays of elation which she has quickly suppressed when she found I was watching her. And on Saturday morning she received a mysterious telephone call which she lied to me about. It was just after we had finished breakfast and normally I'd have left for golf at that hour but I didn't play last Saturday in view of everything that had happened.'

'Does she know that you suspect her?'

'Yes. She made that clear on Saturday.'

'Have you taxed her with it?'

'No. I nearly did. And then I decided not to. Anyway, she'd be bound to deny it.'

'And you've no idea at all who the other man might be?'

'Absolutely none.' He gave Evesham a defeated look. 'But he naturally has a vested interest in my demise.'

'I take it, sir, that you have no objection to my interviewing your wife?'

Mr Ferney shook his head. 'I had hoped to avoid having to tell you any of this, because initially it seemed quite irrelevant. But since Atkins' murder and the receipt of this third letter, I've been having second thoughts. And when just now you asked me whether there was anything in what you euphemistically called my non-official life which might have given rise to these threats, I realised the time had come to tell you.' He paused, then added in a more militant tone, 'I should like your assurance that the information will be treated in strict confidence. I don't want it to get around that I suspect my wife of having found a lover. If it proves to be true, I shall, of course, seek the appropriate remedy in my own time.' He glanced at his watch. 'I must get down to court. Monday morning's always busy with Saturday night's drunk and disorderlies to be despatched.' He rose and walked to the door, Evesham stepping aside to let him pass. 'We shall meet again tomorrow afternoon, Superintendent – if not before.'

'By the way, sir, I'll arrange for your protection to be strengthened,' Evesham said as the magistrate started off down the corridor.

'I'd expect no less,' Mr Ferney flung back.

For just a few minutes in his room he had been almost human, Evesham reflected as he made his way out of the building. But it hadn't taken him long to bounce back as a custom-made bastard.

Some people really did seem cut out to be murder victims.

Evesham had no idea whether he would find Mrs Ferney at home, but he decided it was a risk worth taking rather than forewarn her of his arrival.

It was shortly after half past one when he pulled up outside the house. He walked up the path to the front door and rang the bell. There was a large cherry tree in the front garden and two round flower beds planted with rose bushes.

He was about to ring a second time when he heard someone approaching.

'Mrs Ferney?' he asked the woman who opened the door. She was in her early forties and did nothing to conceal the fact. By no stretch of imagination could she be called pretty, but she had regular features, dominated by a pair of large brown eyes.

'Yes, I'm Mrs Ferney,' she said in a wary voice. 'What do you want?'

It was the tone of someone used to repelling salesmen and pedlars of cranky religions from her doorstep.

'I'm Detective Superintendent Evesham of Scotland Yard, Mrs Ferney . . .'

She gave a small gasp. 'Something's happened to Donald?' Her eyes stared anxiously at him.

'No, nothing's happened to him . . .'

'He told me he'd received threats and then his usher was murdered and we've had an officer keeping watch on the house when Donald's at home.'

Evesham nodded. 'I know. I arranged it.'

'Yes, of course you must know. I'm sorry.'

For half a minute there was silence while she continued staring at him dully.

'I wonder if I might come in. It'll be better if we talk inside.'

She led the way into the drawing-room, a large, airy room with french windows looking out on to the garden at the back.

She walked across and sat down on the edge of the sofa, leaving Evesham to sit where he wanted. He chose a chair opposite her.

'Has your husband spoken to you on the phone since he left home this morning, Mrs Ferney?' She shook her head and he went on, 'Then you'll be unaware that he's received a further threatening letter.'

She stared at him as if mesmerised by his voice and nervously moistened her lips.

'Can you guess why I've come to see you?'

She continued to stare at him as if her brain was no longer in touch with her limbs. Then with an almost painful gesture, she slowly shook her head again.

'Your husband suspects that you're having an affair with another man. Is that true?'

It seemed an age before she spoke and Evesham watched her intently, wondering how she was going to react to the accusation. Anger? Indignation? Confession? Scarcely the last, he reckoned.

'Donald told you that?' she said at last in a voice that sounded as if she had lost the partial use of her vocal chords.

'Yes. And its relevance as far as I'm concerned, Mrs Ferney, is that it might – and I stress might – provide someone with a motive to send him threatening letters.'

'But I thought they were connected with some case he's dealing with.'

'We don't know. That's why we're having to investigate every possibility.'

'And Donald actually told the police that he suspected me of having an affair?' she said in the same stunned tone.

'He told the police in the shape of myself, Mrs Ferney. Now what about an answer to my question?'

'It's nonsense, of course,' she said, meeting his gaze full on.

'Your husband's suspicions are completely unfounded?'

'Completely. I've never been unfaithful to him since we've been married.'

'Is he someone with a naturally suspicious nature?'

'I wouldn't have said so.'

'I wonder why he's become suspicious now? Can you help me about that?'

'I think he's a very worried man. The threats and the usher's murder have upset him much more than he's let on. He's not a demonstrative sort of person. In fact, he's one of those Englishmen who regard it as bad form to show emotion.' She watched her hand as it caressed the arm of the sofa and, without looking up, asked, 'Did he tell you with whom I'm supposed to be having an affair?'

It was obvious that she already knew the answer, for Evesham would not be questioning her at all if he had the name of a supposed lover. This he had all along recognised as the weakness in the hand he had to play.

'No, he didn't,' he replied in a tone sharper than he intended.

'That's a pity. Because if he had, you'd soon be able to disprove his suspicions.'

'How do you and your husband get on, Mrs Ferney?'

'Didn't he tell you?' she asked with a faintly jeering note.

'I'd like to hear what you say.'

'We co-exist.'

'You don't have any children?'

'Unfortunately, no. Things might have been different if we had.' She gave him a look of mild defiance. 'It was my fault. I couldn't conceive. And that's unforgivable in the eyes of some husbands.'

Evesham shifted in his chair and stared thoughtfully at the patterned rug which lay between them.

'Look, Mrs Ferney, supposing we wipe the slate clean of this interview so far and start again . . .' He held up his hand when she seemed about to speak and went on, 'I shall obviously have to go on investigating this aspect. If you've told me the truth, all well and good. But if you haven't and I discover that there is another man in the background, you do realise, don't you, how much worse it will be for him – and possibly for you as well? Because it will appear that you lied to me to conceal his guilt. That's why I'm giving you another chance to tell me the truth. Moreover, I promise that I won't divulge the identity of the person to your husband, provided, of course, he has had nothing to do with the threatening letters or with Atkins' murder. Now, that's a more than fair bargain, Mrs Ferney, so just think carefully for a moment before you reply.'

While he had been speaking, he had observed her increasing nervousness. She plucked incessantly at imaginary specks on the arm of the sofa and frequently passed her tongue over her lips. Evesham watched her, wondering whether he had managed to press the right button. She seemed to be wavering and, at least, he was now in no doubt that her husband's suspicions were well-founded.

At length she looked across at him and said, 'I can only repeat what I've already told you.'

Evesham stood up to go. Gazing down at her, he said, 'Let me give you a final word of advice, Mrs Ferney. Pray hard that your husband doesn't get murdered. Pray very hard.'

CHAPTER 12

The next day, Tuesday, the Wilkley case was due to be resumed in the afternoon and Evesham persuaded Mr Ferney to allow himself to be fetched from home and driven to court in a police car. It was an additional precaution that he deemed advisable on this day in particular.

Though the magistrate clearly expected further protection, he still showed considerable ill-grace in accepting that this involved the physical company of police officers.

The two patrol officers who picked him up in Kew just after nine o'clock the next morning soon gave up any attempt at polite conversation and left him to sit in glowering silence in the back of the car.

They were not to know, of course, of the strained relationship with his wife, which had resulted in the exchange of not more than half a dozen words since he had arrived home the previous evening. She had made no reference to Detective Superintendent Evesham's visit nor had she confronted him about his suspicions. But she had no need to do either. He, for his part, had not taken the opportunity of having a showdown with her. Each, in effect, had retired to the trenches and left the terrain between them unoccupied.

When he had come up to bed that night, it was to find that Rachel was sleeping in the spare-room. They had had single beds for several years so that her move was more symbolic than anything else.

Unaware of the magistrate's entrance in Halfpenny Lane, the driver of the patrol car began to slow down as he approached the main door of the court.

'Take me to the magistrate's entrance,' Mr Ferney said sharply when he realised what was happening.

'Sorry, sir, you'll have to guide me. This is the only entrance to Bloomsbury Magistrates' Court I know,' the driver said stolidly.

'Left and first left again. It's in Halfpenny Lane.'

As they pulled up outside the small open yard at the back of the court building, the co-driver leaned back from the front passenger seat and opened the door. He was damned if he was going to jump out and play the part of a footman.

Mr Ferney got out and with a brief nod of acknowledgement strode toward the magistrate's entrance, while the patrol car shot away with an angry screech of tyres which seemed to express the occupants' view of their passenger. It was only afterwards that they recalled having been instructed not to drive off until they had seen the magistrate safely inside the building.

'Think we better go back, Bill, and make sure he's not stretched out on the ground?' the driver enquired.

'If I thought he was, it'd be worth the journey,' Bill replied.

When Mr Ferney reached his room, he laid his unread *Times* on his desk and, after taking off his hat and coat and satisfying himself that his shoes didn't require a polish, went over to the window and stared across at the empty building on the other side of Halfpenny Lane that was awaiting demolition. It had once been a small bakery with two floors of living accommodation above. When the lease expired, a property speculator bought the premises and the baker moved out. That had been two years ago, since when the new owner had gone bankrupt and the building had been left to decay, a process enthusiastically assisted by vandals. It was a not uncommon situation, but it had always affronted Mr Ferney that it could happen so close to his court and, worse still, within view of his own room. It was for this reason that he had had his desk moved, so that he now sat with his back to the window and didn't see the depressing sight.

He turned away from the window and paced up and down for a few moments, experiencing the nervous restlessness of an athlete before an important race, though he, at least, knew what was in store for him. He was filled only with a sense of general foreboding. He glanced at his watch. It was another half hour before the court was due to sit; another ten minutes before P.C. Shipling would appear with the register showing the morning's list of cases. In a sudden decisive movement he went and sat down at his desk . . .

P.C. Shipling was humming the habanera from *Carmen* as he mounted the stairs to the magistrate's corridor. He had a repertoire of opera pops which he would inaccurately hum to himself as he went about his work. There had been one occasion when, in a forgetful moment one afternoon, he had hummed the soldiers' chorus from *Faust* in the course of a particularly long and dull motoring case. Fortunately, the clerk had given him a sharp look before the magistrate had become aware of the sound. Because he knew that his humming was unmelodious to most ears, it seldom rose above the sound of bees on a summer's day.

As he reached the top of the stairs, he wondered what sort of mood he would find Mr Ferney in. He had heard on the court grapevine about the threats the magistrate had received.

At least he's got guts, he thought to himself. A good many would have disappeared on hasty leave of absence after threats coupled with an obvious intention to kill. Poor old Reg Atkins, it was ironic that he should have met his end through ignoring the magistrate's edict. It had been a heavy price to pay for nothing worse than a bit of childish naughtiness.

Shipling was about half-way along the corridor, his rubber-soled boots squeaking on the polished linoleum, when the magistrate's door was suddenly flung open and Mr Ferney lurched out.

'I've been shot at,' he exclaimed to the astonished Shipling.

In that frozen moment of time, Shipling's trained eye took in the slightly dishevelled hair, the look of shocked disbelief and the smudges of dust on his dark suit. He dashed forward to break the magistrate's fall.

'It's all right, I wasn't hit,' Mr Ferney said, giving himself a slight shake. 'The bullet went somewhere past my right ear.' He began brushing the dust off his trouser knees and the front of his jacket. 'I threw myself on the ground,' he added, as if some explanation was called for.

'You stay here, sir,' P.C. Shipling said, pushing past the magistrate into the room.

The centre pane of the window had a neat hole in it and the glass had starred to its edges all round. The two casement windows on either side were undamaged.

Shipling's gaze went to the wall opposite the window. About four feet up from the floor and immediately below a print of the Law Courts was a small jagged hole round which the paint had flaked off. He could see the bullet embedded about half an inch in. Glancing back at the window, he reckoned the trajectory had been slightly downward, which meant the weapon had probably been fired from the second floor of the building opposite. There was no sign of life at any of its boarded-up windows.

He turned to find the magistrate watching him from the doorway.

'When did this happen, sir?'

'A couple of minutes before you saw me. I was sitting at my desk when suddenly I heard a tinkling of glass and a sort of thump sound as the bullet hit the wall. I immediately threw myself on to the floor and lay there for a minute or so before crawling to the door.'

'You didn't look across at the building opposite?'

'What! And pop up like a target at a fairground shooting competition?'

'No, of course not,' Shipling said quickly. 'I'll phone Detective Superintendent Evesham straight away, sir. Meanwhile, I suggest you come and sit in Miss Purton's room. Have you the key to your door? It had better be locked to preserve the scene.'

Mr Ferney produced a ring of keys from his pocket and locked the door without comment. Then he walked ahead of Shipling to Miss Purton's room at the farther end of the corridor. Opening the door he walked straight in.

'She doesn't appear to have arrived yet,' he said, glancing pointedly at his watch.

'You wait in here anyway, sir, until I come back and tell you what's happening. If I may make a suggestion, sir, you can put over most of the cases to another day and just deal with what's vital. That means you can be in and out of court and available to the police for most of the morning.'

Mr Ferney stared at the jailer but said nothing.

'I'll get Elsie to bring you up a cup of tea, sir,' Shipling added, as he turned to go. That was the best thing for shock, he reflected. That was what they used to give bomb casualties in the war. He suddenly remembered that the afternoon was allotted to the Wilkley case. Ah well, let's first get through the morning was his last thought as he hurried away.

It was five minutes later, at twenty minutes past ten precisely, that the door burst open and Miss Purton came in. She looked out of breath and flustered, but stopped in her tracks at the sight of Mr Ferney sitting in her desk chair.

'I'm sorry, Mr Ferney, I wasn't expecting to see you . . . ,' she stammered, staring at him for an explanation.

'I've taken refuge in your room,' he said, stiffly, 'someone having shot at me in mine.'

'Oh, no! How terrible! Are you all right?'

'I'm happy to say that whoever it was missed.'

'But who . . . how did it happen?'

'The shot came from the building the other side of Half-penny Lane. As to who, I can't tell you. By the time I'd recovered from the shock, I imagine he was well clear of the place. He'd hardly have hung around.'

'Have the police been notified?' she asked anxiously.

'Shipling's attending to that now. I shall adjourn as many of the cases as I can. In that way we should be able to clear the list in half an hour. I obviously need to be on hand when the police come.' He paused and added in a meaning tone, 'I don't doubt that they'll wish to question court staff as well. Find out who was in the building at the time and things like that.'

Miss Purton looked confused. 'I'm afraid I was late arriving this morning. My mother needed attention just as I was leaving the house and I missed my usual train.'

'You'll doubtless tell them that,' Mr Ferney said in a chilly voice.

'You don't really think that any member of the court staff is implicated, do you?' she asked in alarm.

'That's a question for the police. But it'll surprise me if they don't consider every possibility.'

'It's almost unbelievable. First Reg Atkins' death and now this. It's like a bad dream.'

'I can assure you, Miss Purton, that it's anything but a dream to me. It's all disagreeably real.'

'Yes, I didn't mean . . .'

'Hadn't you better go down and get ready for court?' he broke in.

'Are you going to sit right away?' she asked in surprise. 'I thought I made it clear just now that . . .'

'I'm sorry, I didn't understand. I gathered you would wait till the police came.'

'I should like to sit as soon as possible. The police can manage without me for half an hour or so. They can get on with examining my room for a start. By the time they wish to see me, I'll be free.'

'I'll go down immediately and warn everyone what's happening.'

'There's no need to warn anyone of anything! Just go down and I'll follow you in a couple of minutes. Anyway, I've no doubt that the word has already gone round. Shipling will have seen to that.'

After Miss Purton had departed below, Mr Ferney consulted his watch. It was three minutes before half past ten and he was determined to take his seat on the bench at exactly the half hour. That would impress the public. 'Magistrate scorns danger' was the headline he saw in his mind's eye as he got up to go down to court. He had just reached the door when there was a knock and Elsie opened it, a steaming cup of tea in hand.

'P.C. Shipling said to bring you this, sir,' she remarked, gazing at him in a faintly awestruck fashion.

'Not now. I have to go down to court.'

'It'll do you good. Help to steady your nerves,' she said, holding out the tea.

'My nerves are all right, thank you. I'll have one later. But coffee. Black coffee.'

Leaving her standing there, he set off along the corridor.

When the young clerk who was temporarily acting as usher, called out, 'Everyone stand', Mr Ferney had the feeling there were a hundred spotlights trained on him as he walked on to the bench and took his seat. There was certainly no doubt that he had never before been such a focus of attention. Some of the stalwarts of the public gallery gazed at him with the respect normally accorded a sporting hero. He noted, too, that the press box was full and even as he sat down, two more newspapermen thrust their way into court. It didn't take long for a bit of dramatic news to spread through London's grapevine.

A quite unwonted stillness reigned after everyone had sat down. Mr Ferney gazed calmly round the court for a full minute before speaking.

'Owing to circumstances beyond the court's control, I regret that I shall not be able to take a normal morning's list. I propose to put over most cases without hearing any evidence, as I have shortly to leave the bench for the remainder of the morning. I have no reason to doubt, however, that this afternoon's list will proceed as arranged.' He glanced at the press box and then the public gallery. 'I regret causing anyone inconvenience.'

Emboldened by this, one of the newspapermen stood up and said, 'Would you be prepared to talk to the press, sir?'

Inspector Dibben glared at him and motioned him to sit down, but the man stood his ground, encouraged by Mr Ferney's polite gaze.

'I must ask you and your colleagues to be patient. I am sure you will appreciate that my first duty is to assist the police with their enquiries. If it becomes possible to meet you gentlemen later in the day, I will certainly do so, but I can make no promises. It must depend on events.'

The newspaperman nodded. 'Anyway, congratulations on your escape, sir.'

'Thank you very much,' Mr Ferney replied with a gracious smile. 'I am grateful to you for your understanding. I might add that I, personally, have never felt let down by the press. But now we must get on,' he added, glancing in P.C. Shipling's direction.

Evesham and Detective Inspector Cruttenden arrived at

court about the same time which was a few minutes after Mr Ferney had taken his seat.

Before leaving the Yard, Evesham had arranged for Cruttenden to be phoned ten minutes after his own departure. He didn't wish the D.I. to arrive at the court ahead of him. In the event, he had timed it just right.

They met in the jailer's office as P.C. Shipling slipped out of court to marshal his line of defendants. Quickly, he told them what had happened.

'We'd better go straight up to his room,' Evesham said.

'It's locked and he has the key,' Shipling replied 'I'll nip back into court and see if I can get it from him.'

'Then we'll start by going to have a look at the building from which the shot was fired and come back here afterwards. Which is the best way round there?'

'Easiest, sir, if you slip out of the magistrate's door. But you'll have to come all the way round to the main entrance to get back in again.'

'These old courts were built like the Hampton Court maze,' Evesham observed, as he and Cruttenden made their way along corridors and up and down staircases to avoid passing through the public parts of the building.

As they passed the magistrate's room, Evesham tried the door handle to confirm that it was locked. They emerged into the small open yard and noticed a patrol car parked in Halfpenny Lane.

'I've got men posted at each end,' Cruttenden said. 'If you're not quick off the mark, you find the press have stampeded over the scene like a herd of foraging animals before the poor old police ever arrive.'

They reached the pavement and turned to look back at the rear of the court building. The hole in Mr Ferney's window was visible, even without the starred effect.

'The centre pane's a fixed window,' Evesham said. 'Those on either side open outwards.'

D.I. Cruttenden grunted and turned to look at the disused building from which the shot appeared to have been fired. An officer got out of the patrol car and came toward them.

'Nobody been inside?' Cruttenden asked.

'Not since we've been here, sir.'

'Or come out, I suppose?' The officer shook his head.

'I reckon that's the window he must have fired from,' Evesham said, pointing at one on the second floor. 'The court's first floor is higher than this building's and Shipling's impression was that the bullet had a slightly downward path.'

Cruttenden nodded cursorily. 'Better let me lead the way, sir,' he said, moving toward the boarded-up entrance. Watch how I do it, his tone clearly said. There were two loose planks which swung inwards when pushed. 'Think you can manage, sir?' he asked as he eased himself through the gap. 'Try and step in as far as you can. There may be footprints just inside and we don't want to disturb them. Shall I give you a hand?' he added, as he turned to watch Evesham squeeze through.

'I'm not entirely unused to this sort of thing,' Evesham said in a faintly nettled tone, as he joined Cruttenden at the foot of the stairs.

'No offence meant,' Cruttenden remarked as he gripped the bottom of the banister rail which immediately came away in his hand. 'Oh, heck!'

'That means our marksman probably went up on the wall side,' Evesham observed drily. He stooped down to examine the staircase. 'Yes, you can see where the dust has been disturbed. And if I'm not mistaken, he's deliberately scuffed over his shoe-prints.'

'He's sure to have missed one in his hurry to get away,' Cruttenden said, with restored assurance.

'We'll find that out when we have a bit more light on the situation. Got a torch?'

' 'Fraid not, sir.'

'Try the car. They're bound to have one.'

In the grey, half-light within the building, Evesham sensed rather than observed Cruttenden's pique as he clambered back through the gap in the boarded-up doorway. A couple of minutes later, however, he returned with a large black torch.

Standing at the foot of the staircase he focused the beam on each of the first half dozen steps in turn.

'Looks like you said, sir,' he remarked in an almost respectful tone.

'If we go up the banister side, we shan't be treading on any footprints he's left. Lead on.'

They reached the second floor without further event and went into the front room, which had obviously once been a bedroom. A rancid-looking mattress rested against one wall and there was also an ancient chair with its springs sticking up through the torn upholstery.

Cruttenden shone his torch on the floor to reveal what seemed to be a recent disturbance of the dust.

The window, like all the others in the building, was boarded up, but there were large cracks between the slats of rough wood through which light filtered.

Keeping close to the wall, and avoiding the direct path between door and window, they made their way round.

'Yes, this was where he fired from all right,' Cruttenden said keenly, shining his torch on the floor immediately below the window. They could see where the dust had been churned up.

Standing to one side of the window, he leaned across and touched the slats of wood. The third one from him swung away so that he almost lost his balance. It was hinged on a single nail at the top.

'He fired through there, sir,' he said. 'Very handy. Unless anyone was actually looking for the barrel, they'd never see it. He wouldn't have needed to let much more than the muzzle show. Give him a silencer and a telescopic sight and he was as well set up as any marksman could be.'

'Except that he missed.'

'Not by more than an inch or so from what Ferney told Jock Shipling.'

'What would you say the range was? Thirty yards?'

'About that, sir.'

'No sign of the spent case, is there?' The beam of the torch danced across the floor. 'Can't see one.'

'Wouldn't really have expected him to be that careless,' Evesham observed.

From time to time since he had entered the room, he had sniffed hard. He now did so again.

'Would you have expected to smell cordite?' he asked in a faintly puzzled tone.

D.I. Cruttenden also sniffed and appeared to give the matter thought. 'Not necessarily. There's a fine old draught coming through those slats. I imagine that mattress is giving off a fair old pong, but you don't notice it.'

Evesham walked over to the mattress and stooped down to smell it.

'A bit musty,' he remarked, as he straightened up. 'We'd better get forensic here as soon as possible. They'll have a field day. Just like terriers in a corn barn.' He moved across to the door. 'Time we went and examined the receiving end of things. With luck, the magistrate will be out of court by now.'

As he made his way carefully downstairs, he knew there was something he was trying to recall. Something he had seen or been told which was relevant to what had now happened.

It wasn't until he was on the pavement waiting for D.I. Cruttenden to join him that it suddenly came to him.

As a young Detective Constable, Dibben had been trained as a police marksman.

CHAPTER 13

Evesham and Cruttenden were about to set off on the quarter of a mile walk round to the front of the court when they saw P.C. Shipling waving to them from the magistrate's entrance.

'Jock's about the only helpful person there,' Cruttenden observed as they crossed Halfpenny Lane.

'The magistrate's waiting upstairs,' Shipling said when they reached him.

In fact, Mr Ferney was standing at the head of the stairs and came into view as soon as they rounded the bend half-way up.

'Good morning, sir,' Evesham said. 'We've just been across to the building opposite.'

'Find anything?'

'Signs of someone having been there.'

'Any clues?'

'I'm hoping forensic will find a few of those.' He turned to Cruttenden. 'Perhaps you'd go and phone the lab now. We'd better have a ballistics expert as well as the usual. We'll also want a photographer and the fingerprint people.'

Cruttenden nodded unenthusiastically. He had never taken orders too readily and nowadays he was more used to giving instructions than receiving them. Where the hell was one of his sergeants?

'I haven't been back inside my room since locking it immediately after the occurrence,' Mr Ferney said, taking a key from his pocket and stepping up to the door.

Opening it, he moved aside for Evesham to go in first. It

was less a gesture of courtesy than of precaution, the officer felt.

It didn't require an expert to note that the bullet in the wall, the hole in the window and the boarded-up window frame in the building opposite were in alignment. Evesham reckoned that the sniper's aim had been about fifteen degrees below horizontal. The back of the magistrate's head would have been framed in the centre panel of his window.

'Would you mind just sitting in your chair for a moment, sir?' he said. 'I'd like to see the exact position you were in when the shot was fired.'

Mr Ferney's display of reluctance was of someone suddenly called upon to perform a party trick. With an unhappy expression, he walked across to the chair and sat down.

'Were you sitting as upright as that?' Evesham asked, for the magistrate's posture resembled that of a condemned man strapped into the electric chair.

'No, I was probably bent forward.'

'What were you actually doing?'

'I was glancing at my paper.'

'Would your head have been moving?'

'Yes. I had the paper spread open on the desk in front of me, so I moved my head as I glanced down the various columns.'

'Just show me.'

'You don't really want me to open out the paper again, do you?' he said in an edgy voice.

'Not if it's a problem,' Evesham said mildly. 'Just pretend you're reading it.'

Like a bad actor, Mr Ferney leaned forward and went through the motions of scanning the columns of a newspaper.

'Yes, that gives me a good idea of the way your head

was moving. It's what probably saved your life, sir. It was just enough to disturb his aim.'

Evesham walked across to where the bullet had embedded itself in the wall and bent down to examine the hole.

'Looks to me like a .22,' he observed. He turned back to the magistrate who had got up from his chair and was standing beside the door.

'I gather, sir, that you never saw any sign of movement in the building opposite?'

'When?'

'At any time?'

'No.'

'Did you look across after the shot had been fired?'

'No. I got down on the floor.'

'That was very sensible, sir. It's just possible he waited to have a second shot, but I doubt it. Anyway, if you suddenly vanished from his sights, he probably thought he'd hit you. Have you ever noticed anyone showing an interest in the building opposite?'

'No. I'm not given to gazing out of the window. It's a depressing enough view in all conscience. That's why I had my desk turned round, so that I didn't have to see it.'

'We'll have to find out who was in Halfpenny Lane around that time. It's just possible that someone was seen leaving.'

'It's a fairly deserted street.'

'All the more reason for someone to have been spotted and remembered, particularly as he'd have been carrying a bag of some sort. You can't slip a rifle into your jacket pocket.'

'You constantly refer to "he" and "him", Superintendent. Has it occurred to you that it might be a she?'

'Not seriously, sir. Why?'

Mr Ferney's mouth turned down at the corners in an expression of distaste.

'Miss Purton arrived late this morning. It was about ten minutes after the shooting and, what's more, she showed distinct signs of agitation when she found me sitting in her room.'

'Did she say why she was late?'

'She produced the facile excuse that she had missed her usual train because her mother required attention just as she was about to leave the house.'

'But you didn't believe her?'

'I'm merely stating the facts,' Mr Ferney said, with a sniff.

And adding more than a pinch of prejudice too, Evesham reflected. Aloud he said, 'I'll bear it in mind, sir. I thought for one moment you were referring to your wife when you said a "she".'

'My wife couldn't hit a twelve-foot target at point-blank range,' he said dismissively.

'Is that the only reason you exclude her?'

Mr Ferney frowned. 'What are you trying to tell me, Superintendent?' he asked after a thoughtful pause.

'I went to see your wife yesterday afternoon, sir.'

'So I gather.'

'She told you?'

'No. But I knew from her demeanour. Did you learn anything from your visit?'

'She denied that there was another man in her life.'

'That was to be expected. But did she convince you?'

'Let's say, I have an open mind on the subject.'

'That's a luxury *you* can afford,' Mr Ferney remarked, with a further sniff.

'But if she does have a lover, it's become vital to discover his identity.'

'You think it was he who shot at me?'

'Don't you, sir? After all, it was you who told me of your suspicions because you felt they might be relevant to the threats you've received. What's happened this morning is another link in the same chain.'

'I suppose so,' Mr Ferney said in a suddenly defeated tone. He gave Evesham a weary look. 'I'm afraid the strain is beginning to tell a bit. It wouldn't be so bad if one had any idea who's behind all this. And why.'

'If we knew why, we'd almost certainly know who.'

Mr Ferney nodded slowly. 'You've no idea what it's done to me. I now look with suspicion at complete strangers in the street.'

'Think hard, sir. If your wife has taken up with another man, the odds are it's somebody you know. A neighbour or someone met on a holiday. Can't you think of anyone?'

'So you *do* believe she has a lover! Despite your open mind,' he said, with a faint note of triumph.

'Yes, I do. I didn't find her denial very convincing.'

'She's never been a flighty sort of person. She has a number of women friends, but she doesn't find it all that easy to get along with people. I've racked my brains, but can't think of anyone. In one way, it's inconceivable to me that she's got a man hidden away somewhere. I mean, she's never been a very sexual person and she's not the sort of woman men pursue on sight. I just can't believe it. Except that I'm certain it's happened.'

Nobody was better aware than a police officer how little some husbands did know their wives. How often a woman had said to Evesham in the course of an enquiry, 'For God's sake don't tell my husband.' It wasn't always another man either, sometimes it could be secret gambling or persistent shop-lifting. And, of course, it happened the other way about as well. A wife would often have no inkling what her husband got up to. He remembered one couple in their fifties who had been happily married for over thirty years.

Every Saturday afternoon in the winter the husband would go off and watch football. Or so his wife believed, until it transpired he spent the time in different public call boxes phoning obscenities to single ladies whose names he plucked at random from the telephone directory.

'Does your wife have money of her own?' Evesham asked, wondering whether Mr Ferney would deign to confirm what he had heard to this effect.

'Yes, she has,' the magistrate replied in a tone which slammed the door on the subject. Shortly after this, D.I. Cruttenden returned, to be followed half an hour later by a number of experts from the Metropolitan Police Laboratory.

'I suggest you have lunch here, sir,' Evesham said, as he prepared to leave. 'Someone can fetch you sandwiches if that's all right.'

'I'd prefer to go out,' Mr Ferney said stiffly. 'I'm beginning to find the atmosphere here oppressive and claustrophobic. It'll do me good to get some fresh air before I sit this afternoon.'

Evesham frowned. 'Very well, sir. I don't recommend it, but if you insist, I'll arrange for an officer to accompany you.'

'Surely that's not necessary, Superintendent,' Mr Ferney said in an outburst of exasperation. 'I mean, it's hardly likely anyone's going to make another attempt on my life so soon.'

Evesham stared at him in surprise. One moment, he was obsessed with thoughts of lurking danger and now he was proposing to walk around the streets unprotected. Before Evesham could say anything, however, the magistrate spoke again.

'Oh, very well, I'll have sandwiches in my room if that's what you want,' he said like a sulky schoolboy.

Evesham thought it wiser not to point out that he was

going to be dispossessed of his room for, at least, the remainder of the morning and probably longer.

'I took the opportunity of checking on the court staff after I phoned the lab,' Cruttenden said, as he and Evesham made their way along the corridor outside the magistrate's room. In a significant tone he added, 'Miss Purton came in late this morning.'

'I know. She missed her usual train.'

Cruttenden frowned in annoyance at the damp impact of his news.

'You're not suggesting, sir, that we accept that at face value?'

'No; but I wouldn't give it high priority. I don't really see Miss Purton as a murderer and certainly not one who would use, first, a blunt instrument and then the sort of firearm somebody had across the road.'

An obstinate look came over Cruttenden's face. 'Our experience has obviously been different, sir. I've come across quite a number of women who've shot their victims.'

'So have I. But with pistols and revolvers. Not rifles.'

'I once arrested a woman who had taken a shotgun to her husband. Not all that difference between a rifle and a shotgun.'

'Did she lie in wait for him and shoot him as he came up the garden?'

'No, it happend in the kitchen.'

'Exactly. Women don't kill with firearms other than at close quarters. Anyway, what else did you find out?'

'Inspector Dibben also wasn't in at the time it happened. But then I gather that he never arrives until twenty past ten.'

'Have you spoken to him?'

'Yes. The first he knew of it was when he arrived. Jock Shipling told him.'

'What was his reaction?'

'You know Dibben. He doesn't give anything away. He just said something to the effect that if things went on this way, soon they'd all be under siege.'

'No telltale marks on his trousers?'

'If he'd been inside that house this morning, all I can say is that he'd returned via the dry cleaner's.'

One of Cruttenden's sergeants came and joined them at the top of the stairs where they were standing.

'We've searched the house thoroughly, sir,' he said. 'There's nothing of significance there at all. The fingerprint chappie and forensic are still over there.'

'Think I'll go across and see how they're getting on,' Cruttenden said.

Evesham nodded. He certainly had nothing better to suggest. Until they uncovered a motive, they were not going to get anywhere. That became more evident with each day that passed.

Was it really possible, he wondered, for the target of threats and murder attempts to be so totally ignorant of why he was being relentlessly hunted? And then again, was that being quite fair to Mr Ferney? Though some of his suggestions had been a bit wild, Evesham had the impression that the sudden doubts about his wife's fidelity had shaken him considerably and he had been driven, albeit reluctantly, to admit to himself that what had happened had its cause in the private recesses of his domestic life.

The more he had thought about it, the more Evesham had come round to the same viewpoint, if only because it revealed a motive. The threats, together with Atkins' murder and the attempt this morning on the magistrate's life had all been skilfully devised to lay a false trail, to make it appear that they arose from something in Mr Ferney's court life when the opposite was the truth.

As his thoughts ran to their end, he knew what he had to do. Now and without delay. Telephone Mrs Ferney and use the further attempt on her husband's life to shock her into telling him the name of her lover.

He found a phone in an unoccupied room and dialled the number. A strange voice answered, but when he said he wished to speak to Mrs Ferney, he was told to wait. He heard a muffled shout of, 'Mrs Ferney, telephone wants you,' followed by the lifting of an extension receiver.

'Hello.'

'This is Detective Superintendent Evesham, Mrs Ferney. I'm speaking from Bloomsbury Magistrates' Court. There's been another attempt on your husband's life. He was shot at.'

'Oh, my God! Is he all right?'

'Yes, but it was a near thing.'

'You mean he's wounded?'

'No, I mean the bullet only just missed his head.' He heard her let out a quick sigh. 'You sound relieved.'

'I am,' she said dully.

'You remember my parting words to you yesterday, Mrs Ferney?'

'Yes.' Her voice sank to a whisper.

'You didn't pray hard enough, did you? What happened this morning was as close to murder as it could come. I want to know the name of your boy-friend, Mrs Ferney, and I want it now.'

'There's no such person,' she said in an anguished voice.

'I give you the same promise I gave you yesterday,' he went on, 'namely, if he's in the clear I won't divulge his name. Are you listening to me, Mrs Ferney?'

'Yes.'

'Well?'

'You're wrong, all wrong.'

'In what way?'

'In every way,' she cried out in a tone of weary helplessness.

He waited for her to continue, but only silence followed her outburst.

'It's your duty to assist me. Your duty to your husband and, if you don't rate that very highly, your duty as an ordinary citizen.'

'The police are always reminding people of their duties as citizens,' she said.

'People in your position, Mrs Ferney, shouldn't need reminding.'

'I'm sorry I can't help you any further.'

'Can't or won't?'

'What's it matter? You'll believe what you want to believe.'

'Look, Mrs Ferney, I'm convinced that there is another man in your life and your refusal to tell me his name can only give rise to a most sinister inference. You're shielding him because you know what he's done. To put it bluntly you could be shielding a murderer, which means you could find yourself charged as an accessory.'

'I told you that you'd believe what you wanted to believe,' she said after a pause. 'Anyway, my husband has always told me that no one is under a legal duty to talk to the police. I've done nothing wrong and you can't frighten me the way you probably can some of the people you question.'

'All I am trying to do, Mrs Ferney, is impress upon you the serious consequences that may ensue if you don't assist me. There's such a thing as a moral duty, even if it's not a legal one. And, frankly, I'm surprised that you, the wife of a Metropolitan stipendiary magistrate, should adopt such an obstructionist attitude. I can only draw my own conclusion.'

'Have you finished talking at me?'

For answer, Evesham replaced the receiver. The call had got him nowhere other than to confirm Mrs Ferney's obduracy. Frightenend people became obstinate and there was no doubt she was frightenend. Frightenend of what? Not that her husband was on someone's murder list, but rather that the identity of his would-be killer might become revealed. She was frightened for the murderer, not for the victim.

He closed the office door behind him and made his way down to the ground floor. It was coming up to twelve o'clock. Were it not for the fact that he had to be in court for the Wilkley case all the afternoon, he'd have driven out to Kew now and had a face to face showdown with her. The telephone was never a satisfactory means for serious interrogation. He reckoned that if he couldn't crack her in the course of a direct confrontation, he might as well apply for some pen-pushing job at the Yard, for he would obviously have lost his skill as an interrogator. But police interrogators, like cross-examiners in court, need material on which to work and this is what he lacked vis à vis Mrs Ferney. As an intelligent woman, she had been quick to realise this, so all she'd had to do was ride out the storm. She had now successfully done this twice, but she wouldn't be so fortunate a third time, he determined.

Nevertheless, it was in a mood of deep frustration that he reached the bottom of the stairs. A frustration increased by the fact that, despite all his efforts, he had come no nearer to solving the mystery of Reg Atkins' missing hours. All enquiries in this direction had petered out. Not a soul had come forward with so much as a tenuous thread of information.

He stepped on to the pavement in front of the court and looked across at Philip Smeech's office. He had not previously noticed that you could actually see the solicitor at work at his desk in a first-floor window.

At this moment, he was engaged in an earnest telephone conversation, in which his caller seemed to be doing most of the talking. Evesham could observe his deeply concentrated expression as he listened, biting worriedly at a thumbnail.

It must be a constant struggle, he reflected, trying to maintain ethical standards when you spent your time representing villains, who expected you to adopt every devious ploy on their behalf.

Philip Smeech seemed more successful than many in this respect.

Evesham sucked in a deep lungful of polluted air and went back inside the court building.

CHAPTER 14

'Guess who?' said the voice jovially on the phone.

Betsy had no need to guess. She would recognise Vic Wilkley if he only hiccuped.

'What do you want?' she asked coldly.

'That's not the tone to use to a friend.'

'What do you want?' she repeated.

'I'm back in court again this afternoon.'

'What's that got to do with me?'

'I thought I'd remind you. Remember our little talk last week.'

'I'm not coming to court if that's what you're after.'

'I haven't asked you to, have I? I was just calling for a bit of a friendly chat.'

'It's a bad time.'

'Come off it, Betsy, don't tell me that old cow, Madeleine, is up and about yet! I can hear her snoring from here.'

'What is it you want?' she asked in a tone in which annoyance and anxiety were blended.

'Nothing – yet. But I may need your help later on. Like I said. Remember?'

She let out a quiet sigh of relief. At least he didn't appear set to embroil her in anything immediately. The longer she could hold him off the better. She had no idea in what way she could help him, but this merely increased her fear. Vic Wilkley was as ruthless as any of the crooks he had played along with and, when it suited him, framed. Once he decided to use her, there was no pressure he would not stoop to bring. Moreover, he was well aware of her Achilles heel.

Michael. She thought that if he involved Michael, she would kill him and enjoy doing so.

'Are you still there, Betsy?'

'Yes.'

'You suddenly went very silent.'

'I was thinking.'

'Are you going to wish me luck this afternoon?'

'Do you need it?'

He let out a disagreeable laugh. 'Not as much as you do, perhaps.'

'Will the case finish today?'

'Can't do. Luckily for you. That toady, Detective Superintendent Evesham, will be in the box this afternoon. By the way, have you heard that Ralph Tremler's big ape has disappeared?'

'Big ape?'

'Ruby Huxey, who else?'

'No, why should I have heard? I keep on telling you I've not been in touch with Ralph for years. That's why I don't see how I can help you.'

'Don't you worry about that. When the time comes, I'll tell you quick enough. Anyway, Ruby's gone to ground. The rumour is that he killed the usher outside Bloomsbury Court. On Ralph's instructions, of course.'

Betsy's expression became puzzled in a way that would have aroused Wilkley's interest if he could have seen it.

'Why should Ralph want to kill the usher?'

'He didn't. The big ape killed the wrong man. He meant to get the magistrate.'

'But why?' she asked in a mystified voice.

'Ralph wants to opt out, but without saying so.'

'If he does that, it means you get off.'

'You might sound a bit happier about it, Betsy. After all, it's also in your interest.'

'But how would killing the magistrate help? Wouldn't they start again in front of another?'

'It would mean delay. Long delay. And anything could happen. *Anything*, Betsy.'

Betsy made a rude face at the receiver. She wouldn't be surprised if Vic Wilkley hadn't engineered the whole thing; if it wasn't he who had put about the rumour that Huxey had murdered the usher. He was as devious as the devil himself.

After he had rung off, she glanced at the clock. Soon Madeleine would be stirring which would mean there'd be little peace for the rest of the day.

Betsy got up and walked over to the budgerigar's cage.

'Daft little bugger, aren't you?' she said, gazing at the small green creature which fluttered futilely from one perch to the other. 'But at least you don't have problems.'

When she was in a particularly good mood, she would let it out and it would flutter about the room making small messes in the excitement of its liberty. But there was no question of that today. She had been thinking hard for the past couple of days and had still to decide how to act on what she had found out. Or rather on what she had pieced together.

For Betsy thought she knew who had killed Reg Atkins.

CHAPTER 15

Philip Smeech stared out of his office window at the stunted Gothic facade of Bloomsbury Magistrates' Court. It was the last place he wanted to spend the afternoon. Everything about it had become utterly distasteful to him and defending Sergeant Wilkley merely added to his feeling of antipathy.

It had been his secretary who had burst into his room not long after his arrival to say that an attempt had been made on Mr Ferney's life, but that he was uninjured. If this wasn't shock enough, there had been Rachel Ferney's long telephone call to tell him of Evesham's renewed effort at breaking her. He had found it difficult to dredge up words of exhortation and comfort when he felt his own confidence on the verge of cracking. He was appalled at the manner in which things had got out of hand. Events seemed to have slipped out of his control and, despite realising the vital need to resume it, he had the helpless feeling that too many chain reactions had been established.

His internal telephone gave a buzz and he reached out for the receiver, only to pick up the wrong one in his distracted mood.

'Mr Wilkley's here,' his secretary announced. 'He says he'd like to see you before court.'

Damn the fellow's impertinence, just walking in like that and assuming his solicitor would drop everything and see him. In fact, the only thing he had to drop was the *Daily Telegraph* with whose crossword he was trying to calm his thoughts; but Wilkley was not to know that. Moreover, it was a quarter to two when he might reasonably have been expected to be out at lunch.

'Very well,' he said, making his displeasure apparent. 'Send him in.'

A few seconds later, the door opened and Detective Sergeant Wilkley entered.

'Afternoon, Mr Smeech,' he said in his normal hearty tone. 'What's all this about someone trying to shoot Mr Ferney?'

'You probably know as much about it as I do. I know only what my secretary has told me.'

'All I've seen is a couple of lines in the stop press of a midday paper.'

'I understand,' Smeech said in a tone that sought to put distance between himself and events, 'that someone tried to shoot him through the window of his room. The someone being in the disused bakery opposite the rear of the court.'

'But who was this enterprising someone?'

'I don't think it's an occasion for flippancy.'

'Sorry, I didn't mean to shock you, but who tried to snuff him?'

'If the police know, I certainly don't.'

'You haven't been across at court this morning?'

'I had no occasion to go.'

'I'd have thought this was occasion enough to find out what had happened.'

'I had no wish to get in the way,' Smeech said coolly.

Sergeant Wilkley raised a sardonic eyebrow and glanced out of the window.

'You must be thankful his room doesn't look out this side.'

'Meaning?'

'You'd have had the police swarming over your office quickly enough.' Before Smeech could make any comment,

Wilkley went on, 'Is Superintendent Evesham still leading the enquiry?'

The solicitor bit his lip. 'As far as I know, yes.'

Sergeant Wilkley seemed to brood on the information for a time, his face in repose heavy-featured and as amiable as that of a constipated bull.

'There can be only one reason,' he said, glaring out of the window, 'they think I've had something to do with all the funny goings-on.'

'Not necessarily.'

'Explain.'

'The funny goings-on, as you call them, began with the magistrate receiving a couple of threatening letters. One arrived on the day after our first hearing and the second on our remand date last week. I understand a third arrived yesterday. In those circumstances, they may have thought there was some connection between your case and the sending of the threats.'

'You spell it out very delicately, Mr Smeech, but I've got enough trouble on my plate without being suspected of trying to scare off the magistrate. Though God knows how that's meant to benefit me! Even wonder-boy Evesham must be hard put to make sense out of that.'

'I said a connection between your case and the threats, not you personally.'

'I heard what you said, but I'd like you to make a disclaimer in open court this afternoon.'

The solicitor shied like a startled horse. 'What sort of disclaimer?'

'Saying I've had absolutely nothing whatsoever to do with the sending of any threatening letters to the magistrate nor with the murder of the usher or the shooting this morning.'

Smeech shook his head vigorously. 'There's no call for such a disclaimer and it'd be most unwise. No one's suggested your involvement . . .'

'Yes, they have. By putting Evesham on the case.'

'That's not sufficient reason for making the sort of statement you suggest. Anyway, the magistrate would stop me before I reached the end of the first sentence. And what are the press and public going to make of it? You'd merely be stirring up speculation.'

A stubborn look came over Sergeant Wilkley's face. 'I don't agree.'

'I'm sorry, but I decline to make such a statement. At least, let's see where we stand at the end of the prosecution's case.' He looked at his watch. 'It's time to go across to court.' He rose and picked up his briefcase.

For a while, Wilkley didn't move, but stood staring seemingly at nothing, his lower lip thrust aggressively out.

'You've got all the points I want put to Evesham in cross-examination?' he asked abruptly, emerging from his reverie.

Philip Smeech pretended not to have heard as he opened the door of his secretary's room to speak to her.

When they arrived, they found the vestibule of the court thronged with people. As 'R. v. Wilkley' was the only case listed for the afternoon, it was a safe assumption that they had been drawn by that event and were looking for a contest as full of incident as those seen in Roman arenas of ancient times. It was not difficult to distinguish the press from the general public as they all waited to be admitted into court. There was no doubt that the prospect of seeing Mr Ferney on the bench added to the general air of expectancy and there were one or two who were doubtless praying that a further dramatic attempt on his life might yet take place in court. After all someone had produced a shotgun and threatened the magistrate at West London Court a few years back. But, of course, he had been an American and the British were less spectacular in such matters. They usually confined their murderous assaults to quieter reaches outside the court.

Four uniformed constables suddenly appeared from the corridor leading to the jailer's office and took up positions beside the doors leading into the court-room.

At least they weren't taking any chances, Smeech reflected bleakly. No one was going to get in without being searched.

A newspaperman broke away from those now thrusting toward the entrances and came across to where the solicitor and his client were hovering.

'Afternoon, Mr Smeech. Hello, Vic. Likely to get a few sparks flying this afternoon, are we?'

'You'll have to wait and see,' Smeech said and turned away.

'Won't he be having a go at Evesham?' the man went on unabashed, addressing Sergeant Wilkley.

'Piss off,' Wilkley retorted, baring his teeth in a mirthless smile and following his solicitor toward the jailer's corridor.

P.C. Shipling stood waiting at the door half-way down, which led into court. 'Sorry, Mr Smeech, but orders are everyone has to be searched. Even you learned gentlemen.'

Smeech handed the officer his brief-case and then submitted to being patted for a concealed weapon.

'Like entering the Hilton Hotel,' Wilkley observed, when his turn came.

'I wouldn't know. Park Lane's off my social beat,' Shipling said.

Wilkley frowned angrily. Who was the bloody jailer at Bloomsbury Magistrates' Court to snub him! Serve him right if he suddenly brought his knee up into the man's groin as he bent forward to search him. Accidental like, of course. Fortunately, the prospect of doing so proved sufficiently satisfying and the temptation passed.

Philip Smeech took his seat and nodded to Jude, the prosecuting counsel, who was already in his place.

'I'll be calling Detective Superintendent Evesham,' Jude

said. 'I doubt whether we shall get any further than that this afternoon; assuming, that is, that you cross-examine.'

Smeech merely nodded again. He looks exhausted, thought Jude, wonder what he's been up to.

Further speculation on the cause of Philip Smeech's worn appearance was forestalled by Mr Ferney's entrance into court. Apart from a quick, anxious glance around, he appeared to be his normal composed and dapper self. His errant lock of hair was firmly in place and only an occasional nervous flick of his eyes suggested that anything amiss had happened.

'Yes, Mr Jude, are you ready to proceed?' he asked, then frowned as he became aware of hissed whispers in the solicitor's row in front of him. 'Your client seems to be trying to attract your attention, Mr Smeech.'

'It's nothing, sir,' Smeech replied, half-turning his back on Sergeant Wilkley who was plucking at his sleeve.

'In which case, perhaps you would ask him to keep quiet,' Mr Ferney remarked.

'Are you going to or not?' Wilkley hissed at his solicitor.

'Will you kindly remain silent?' Mr Ferney said sternly, and then transferred his gaze from the defendant to Smeech. 'Unless he can behave himself properly, I shan't allow him to sit beside you. What is it he wants?'

'It's nothing, sir. I'm sorry for the interruption.'

'He still appears to be in disagreement with you over something.'

'That's right, sir,' Sergeant Wilkley said, jumping to his feet. 'I wish to make a statement to the court.'

'Will you kindly sit down and behave yourself?'

'I've decided that I wish to defend myself, sir. I no longer require Mr Smeech's services.'

Smeech looked up at his client with a mixture of indignation and embarrassment. Then also rising to his feet, he said, 'I'm sorry, sir . . . I had no idea this was going to happen.'

'So I perceive from your demeanour.' Turning to Sergeant Wilkley once more, the magistrate went on, 'The court cannot force you to be legally represented, but are you sure you're being sensible in casting your solicitor aside at this juncture? There can be no question of an adjournment.'

'I'm not asking for any adjournment, your worship. I'm quite ready to go on with the case this afternoon and conduct my own defence.'

'You fully understand that you'll be given no special latitude in doing so. I shan't allow you to explore any irrelevant byways.'

'I'm as conversant with the rules of evidence, your worship, as most members of the learned profession.'

'Well, Mr Smeech?' Mr Ferney said, with a distinct note of enjoyment in his tone.

'In the circumstances, sir, I have no alternative but to withdraw from the case,' the solicitor said stiffly.

'No, I don't think you have,' the magistrate observed with a small, frosty smile.

With all eyes upon him, Philip Smeech gathered his papers together and stuffed them into his brief-case. Then, giving Mr Ferney a briskly formal bow, he stalked out.

'May I now make my statement, your worship?' Sergeant Wilkley asked.

Mr Ferney frowned. 'What statement?'

'About all the rumours going around, your worship.'

'This court is not concerned with rumours,' Mr Ferney said firmly.

'But they prejudice me, your worship. I want to make it clear . . .'

The magistrate held up an imperious hand. 'The less you say the better, Sergeant Wilkley. As far as I'm concerned, the only thing that counts is the evidence. Now let us try and get on. We've already lost ten minutes . . .'

'All I want to make clear, your worship, is that I've had absolutely nothing to do with any of the recent events at this court.'

Sergeant Wilkley's tone had reminded Evesham of a runaway steamroller. Nothing was going to stop him, not even the magistrate's look of cold fury. Mr Ferney now glared at him as he sat down and continued to do so for a full half-minute, while Wilkley pretended to study some papers he produced from his jacket pocket.

'Should you see fit to treat the court to another outburst of that nature, you will, I trust, not be surprised to find your bail rescinded at the end of the afternoon.'

Sergeant Wilkley looked up sharply. This was clearly a prospect he had not envisaged. Indeed, he knew as well as did Mr Ferney that it would be a most improper reason for keeping him in custody. But that didn't exclude the possibility, for magistrates could be despots at will in their own small world.

Detective Superintendent Evesham had watched Philip Smeech's departure with a feeling of despair and the prospect of now being cross-examined by Sergeant Wilkley in person filled him with dread. It was not that he felt unable to stand up for himself, it was the introduction of the personal element into their confrontation. He could only hope that Mr Ferney would show the same measure of authority he had been displaying during the past few minutes. You certainly had to hand it to him. No one would have deduced from his recent performance that he was working under an intense nervous strain. It went to show, Evesham supposed, that, given the right incentive, everyone could rise to an occasion. In the magistrate's case, the incentive was to earn the admiration of press and public and show that he was undaunted by everything that had happened. He was still the firm but kindly magistrate of Bloomsbury Court. Admittedly there had been nothing kindly in his treatment of Sergeant Wilkley, but then he had obviously judged that the suspended Vice Squad officer had little popular support in his court.

A few moments later, Evesham was called into the witness box and took the oath, watched by the magistrate who gave no indication that they had ever met before. Miss Purton for her part had her eyes glued to her desk, while Inspector Dibben kept his fastened suspiciously on the press bench in an expression of ill-concealed dislike.

As he put down the testament, Evesham glanced round the court and wondered which of them, if minded, could help him solve what was proving to be a baffling series of crimes. The odds were that one, at least, could give him vital information. But which one? And why had it not already been forthcoming? And what was one to think of a woman who blankly refused to help the police, even though it might result in the forfeiture of her husband's life? And why couldn't he find out where Reg Atkins had spent those unaccounted for hours in the last week of his life, in particular on the evening before his death? Someone knew all right.

He became aware that Mr Jude was looking at him in a speculative manner. Heaven knows what his expression had been as one frustrating question followed the next through his mind.

'Are you with me, Superintendent?' Jude enquired gently.

'Yes, sir . . . I'm sorry . . . would you mind repeating your question?'

'I haven't asked it yet. I was waiting for your attention.'

'Oh do get on with it,' Mr Ferney broke in, 'and stop playing parlour games.'

Evesham's evidence was long and, from the point of view of press and public, almost totally without interest. It comprised, in the main, two long interviews with Sergeant Wilkley at which a string of allegations were put to him.

At the first, his replies had consisted of a series of denials such as, 'rubbish', 'nonsense', 'another whopping lie' and 'perjury comes as easily to him as pissing'. This last reply produced a few happy smiles in the public gallery, but otherwise there was hardly anything worthy of their attention as Evesham ploughed steadily on and Miss Purton recorded his testimony.

And when it came to the second interview which had taken place two weeks later, there was even less of interest, for Wilkley had been accompanied by his solicitor and, on his advice, had answered each allegation with a curt, 'I don't wish to comment.' The fact that he had managed to invest the phrase with a wide range of feeling was lost when it came to repetition in the witness box.

It took just over an hour for Evesham to complete his evidence-in-chief, by which time an atmosphere of torpor hung over the court as if everyone had been quietly tranquillised. It was only the prospect of hearing him cross-examined by Sergeant Wilkley in person that sustained most people's determination to remain.

When at last Mr Jude sat down, the revivifying effect was immediate and interest noticeably perked up.

Mr Ferney gave Sergeant Wilkley a half-hearted nod and he rose, clutching a sheaf of notes.

'Is it true you had to force Mr Tremler to give evidence?' he asked in a belligerent tone.

'No. Mr Tremler made his statement entirely voluntarily.'

'I'm not talking about his statement. Didn't you have to force him to come to court last week?'

'That's not true.'

'I suggest that he didn't want to give evidence, but you twisted his arm.'

'No.'

'Didn't you tell him that if he refused to give evidence, he could find himself back in prison?'

'I certainly did not.'

'Do you agree that he gave the impression of being a reluctant witness?'

'I doubt whether my impressions are of any evidential value.'

'And I uphold that,' Mr Ferney broke in.

'Mr Tremler's a man with a criminal record, isn't he?'

'That was established last week,' Mr Ferney said, before the witness could answer. 'There's no need to go over the same ground again.'

'Well, is he also a well-known figure in Soho?'

'Depends on what you mean by well-known.'

'Are you trying to evade answering the question?' Wilkley asked in a sneering tone.

'No.'

'Answer it then.'

Evesham gave a shrug and glanced at the magistrate who merely stared back at him.

'I suppose he's known to other people in the same line of business, if you call that well-known.'

'To other pornographers and people engaged in vice?'

'If you like.'

'And to the police?'

'Certainly.'

'Is he a man you trust?'

'I don't think I can answer that.'

'Why not?'

'It's not a question within my province as investigating officer.'

They both looked toward Mr Ferney, who gave the appearance of one closely following a Tom and Jerry cartoon.

When it became clear that he was not going to intervene

with a ruling, Evesham added, 'I have no reason to distrust him in respect of any of the matters in this case.'

'You mean you wouldn't trust a word he spoke unless it happened to be against me.'

'I didn't say that.'

'But it's what you meant, wasn't it?'

'I've given you my answer and have nothing to add.'

'No, come on, Superintendent, don't be coy. Isn't that what you meant?'

'I have nothing to add to my previous answer.'

Sergeant Wilkley looked toward the magistrate. 'Perhaps you will make him answer my question, sir.'

'But he considers that he has answered it,' Mr Ferney said blandly. 'I can't force him to say what you want to hear. And, anyway, have you not made your point?'

'If you think so, sir, then I'm satisfied.'

'It doesn't assist you to get into an argument with the witness,' Mr Ferney went on.

'It's difficult not to when he's so evasive.'

'I resent that, sir,' Evesham said angrily. 'I have not been evasive.'

'Merely discreet, I'm sure,' the magistrate observed in a tone of cynical detachment.

Wilkley studied his notes for several seconds. 'You're attached to A10 at Scotland Yard, aren't you?' he asked, without looking up.

'Yes.'

'And that's the branch which investigates complaints against the police, isn't it?'

'Yes.'

'Then what are you doing investigating a murder?' he enquired with a note of triumph.

'Are you referring to the death of the court usher?'

'You know I am.'

'I was instructed to liaise with the divisional officer in charge of the case.'

'Why?'

'Why was I instructed? You'll have to ask my superiors.'

'There he is being evasive again,' Wilkley jeered, looking at Mr Ferney.

But this time the magistrate was looking anything but benign.

'What is the relevance of that line of cross-examination?' he asked in a voice of judicial chill.

'It shows there's prejudice against me, your worship. That the police are trying to load their case.'

'I don't follow.'

'They're as good as suggesting that I had something to do with the usher's murder.'

'The death of the usher and the charges of corruption which you're facing have no evidential connection at all so far as this court is concerned. And I refuse to let you cross-examine the witness on those lines.'

'Am I not entitled to cross-examine him to show that the police are biased against me?' Wilkley asked, bullishly.

Mr Ferney turned toward Evesham. 'Are the police biased against this defendant?'

'No, sir.'

'There, you have his answer,' the magistrate said, turning back to Sergeant Wilkley.

'He was bound to say "no" when it was put to him like that,' Wilkley protested.

'I hope you're not going to argue with *me*.'

'I'm only trying to get fairness.'

'I hope I'm never less than fair.'

'I don't mean you, your worship. I mean from the Commissioner and from Superintendent Evesham who represents him in this case.'

'Have you any further questions to ask the witness?' Mr Ferney asked in a meaning tone.

Sergeant Wilkley glowered at his notes and quickly shuffled several pages.

'Would I be in order to ask for an adjournment, your worship?'

'For what purpose?'

'To prepare my further cross-examination of the witness. After all, it's come on me a bit suddenly.'

'And whose fault is that? It was you who dispensed with your solicitor's services. And I did warn you.'

'I realise that, your worship, but, in my experience, it's usual for courts to give every assistance to defendants in person.'

Evesham looked at the magistrate and saw him wavering. It had been a shrewd thrust. The last thing Mr Ferney would want would be to tarnish his image for fairness with the public.

'What length of adjournment do you have in mind?' he asked.

'I could be ready tomorrow, your worship.'

'And how much longer is your cross-examination of the witness likely to last?'

'Not more than an hour if I have time to prepare myself.'

'An hour?' Mr Ferney said in a scandalised voice.

'Perhaps, I could cut it to half an hour, your worship.'

'Does the court have a spare half-hour tomorrow?' the magistrate asked Miss Purton, who glanced round at P.C. Shipling.

The jailer dashed out of court and returned a minute later with two large official diaries.

'It's your matrimonial afternoon, sir,' he said. 'It doesn't look too heavy. It could be through by half past three.'

'Very well then, I'll remand this case until tomorrow. Not before three o'clock.'

'Same bail, sir?' Shipling asked.

Mr Ferney gave Sergeant Wilkley a long, hard stare. 'Yes I'll renew his bail,' he said, as if it had been a touch and go decision.

'Can you manage tomorrow afternoon?' Jude asked Evesham as the court cleared.

'I wasn't aware I had any choice,' Evesham replied disgustedly.

'It's the helluva nuisance for me, too. I'm in a part heard at Lambeth tomorrow afternoon. I suppose someone'll have to cope with that as best they can. I wish to God he'd never sacked Smeech. Defendants in person can waste more time than a bus driver with a grudge against the public.'

As far as Evesham was concerned, the afternoon had been a complete waste of time. It might have been that, anyway, but it wouldn't have left him feeling quite so out of sorts with the world in general. It was without any pleasure that he decided a sense of duty required him to go and see Mr Ferney in his room and make sure that the car had come to take him home. He was about to make his way out of court when P.C. Shipling returned.

'One of Mr Cruttenden's men has just been on the phone, sir. Asked me to tell you that Huxey's surfaced and the D.I.'s got him at the station now.'

'Good luck to them both,' Evesham muttered sourly after Shipling had dashed out again.

He found Mr Ferney sitting in an armchair over in a corner of his room. He was scarcely recognisable as the autocrat in court of ten minutes earlier. His face was grey with fatigue and he was slumped in the chair with his arms dangling over the sides.

Evesham thought at first that he must have been taken ill.

'It's a reaction to the day's events,' Mr Ferney said in a tired voice, as he read Evesham's thoughts. 'I've seldom felt so drained of vitality.'

'Then you'll be glad to be driven home, sir,' Evesham remarked a trifle sardonically. He glanced at the centre frame of the window which had been covered with a piece of plywood. The ballistics man had presumably removed the broken pane for more detailed examination.

'I'm afraid the car won't be here until four-thirty, sir. I didn't know, of course, that we'd be rising early.'

'I'm afraid I didn't have any choice. I could hardly refuse Wilkley's application in the circumstances.'

Evesham was certainly in no mood to agree, so said nothing.

There was a knock on the door and Inspector Dibben appeared.

'Yes, what is it, Inspector?' Mr Ferney asked from the depths of his chair.

'It's a message for the superintendent,' Dibben said with a stony expression. He turned to Evesham. 'A woman came through on my outside line, wanted to speak to you. Said she had some information to give you. I asked her for her number and said you'd call her back, but she wouldn't give it me. I told her to ring you later at Scotland Yard, but she said she wouldn't be able to phone again till tomorrow morning.'

'Doesn't sound very important, but thanks, anyway,' Evesham said. 'If I'm not in tomorrow morning, I'll arrange for someone to take the call. I wonder why she can't phone again this evening?'

'She said something about being at work and not being able to talk freely. But she did give me her name. Or rather a name.'

Dibben paused giving Evesham a rather strange look.

'What name?'

'Betsy.'

'Betsy? Betsy who?'

'Just Betsy.'

Evesham shook his head. 'It doesn't mean anything to me.'

'Anyway, that was the message,' Dibben said in the same expressionless voice and departed.

'Probably another crank,' Evesham observed. 'Murder investigations attract them like magnets.'

But Mr Ferney made no comment and had, meanwhile, closed his eyes.

CHAPTER 16

Betsy felt anxious and ill-at-ease. It had not gone as she had anticipated. The officer to whom she had spoken had merely said he was the court inspector and had declined to give her his name. He had sounded cold and detached and though he had said he would pass on her message, she had been left with a feeling of dissatisfaction. Instead of having talked to the king-pin and had her doubts and worries removed, they had merely been increased. The only consolation was that the die remained uncast. She could still back-track, for there was nothing to compel her to phone Scotland Yard the next day. They had no way of getting in touch with her, even if they wanted to. They must receive hundreds of anonymous and semi-anonymous calls which were never followed up. She would sleep on it and decide in the morning. Meanwhile, however, she was left feeling flat.

'Was that a client on the phone?' Madeleine asked from the doorway.

'When do you mean?'

'Just now, when Billy was here.'

Billy was one of Madeleine's regulars. He came at half past three on the second Tuesday of each month. He had a small goatee beard and had been christened Billy by Betsy on that account.

'I heard you talking above Billy's puffing.'

'You should concentrate more on your work,' Betsy replied.

Madeleine's ears were as sharp as her money sense and Betsy had long learnt to lower her voice when making private calls on the phone in her front room.

'Now I come to think of it, I never heard the phone ring, so it must have been you making the call.'

'It was.'

'Who were you talking to?'

'Don't I have any private life?'

'Not on my phone, ducky.'

'What's made you mean all of a sudden?'

'Long conversations on my phone can keep clients off the line.'

'If they want to see you enough, they won't mind waiting and trying again,' Betsy said with a note of impatience. Madeleine was constantly getting bees in her bonnet and they invariably concerned money.

'Anyway, who were you talking to?' Madeleine went on in a tone of friendly interest.

'Michael.'

'Isn't he at school today?'

'He thought he'd be back early this afternoon. I wanted to make sure everything was all right.'

Madeleine let out a gusty laugh. 'You're a rotten liar, ducky. But never mind, don't tell me if you don't want to. Let it be another of the little secrets you store away like a squirrel's nuts.'

Betsy shrugged. Madeleine always enjoyed teasing her, but it didn't worry her in the slightest. Just occasionally she was needled but Madeleine was swift to recognise the symptoms and would quickly lay off.

Madeleine now came into the room and walked over to the budgerigar's cage. She stuck a finger through the bars of the cage.

'You look mopey, Fred,' she remarked. 'I don't wonder if you have to listen to Betsy on the phone all day.'

At that moment, the phone rang and Madeleine turned to watch Betsy answer it. She knew at once that it was a client.

'No, I'm the maid,' Betsy said primly. 'That's right, her name's Madeleine . . . Depends on what sort of treatment you require . . . That would be at least £50 . . . In half an hour? Yes, that would be all right . . . You have the address? Fine . . . See you then, John.'

'Another John?' Madeleine said as Betsy replaced the receiver.

'Another John Smith,' Betsy replied drily.

'No marks for imagination.'

'It's other marks he's interested in. Go and get your whips ready.'

Madeleine made a face and sighed.

'You know I don't really go for that,' she said, with a slight pout.

'What I know is that you go for anything with money attached,' Betsy observed. 'And it's fifty quid for very little extra effort.'

Madeleine grinned and departed to her bedroom.

The remainder of the day was taken up with a brisk succession of clients which kept Madeleine busier than she had been for several weeks. She barely had time for her usual early-evening Scotch.

Just before ten o'clock she appeared in the doorway of Betsy's room dressed to go out.

'Put up the shutters, ducky, we're going out for a drink. I've had enough for one day.'

She walked over to the drawer in which Betsy kept the money and took out two £20 notes.

'One for you and one for me,' she said. 'We've earned a bonus. At least, I have.'

Betsy would have preferred to have gone straight home, but it was difficult to refuse in the circumstances and to have done so would have set Madeleine off on one of her recriminative outbursts. She had always regarded her offers of a drink as regal commands.

Happily, they had not long been in the bar before a friend of Madeleine's came in and joined them, which enabled Betsy to make her departure.

'Not going to be late tomorrow, are you?' Madeleine called out as she made her farewells and turned to go.

Betsy frowned. 'Why?'

'You sometimes are after one of your mysterious phone calls.'

'I'll be in by one.'

'Why not twelve?'

'I may be.'

'Give it a try, ducky.'

Betsy's journey back to Fulham involved a change of bus in the King's Road, the second bus decanting her at the end of the street in which she lived.

She was still trying to decide what to do the next day when she got off the bus and turned to walk the last quarter of a mile. She was a night person and it never worried her being out alone late. And her home street was so familiar that its dim lighting gave her a feeling of hearthlike cosiness. She would have hated it if the council had erected new lighting that gave everyone complexions like cadavers fished out of the river.

She quickened her step, hoping that Michael would still be up. It would depend on what sort of day he had had and whether there was anything on television he wanted to see. But she was a bit earlier than usual, so it was possible he hadn't yet gone to bed. He had recently acquired a girl-friend, but Betsy had persuaded him to see her only at weekends. Luckily her parents were equally sensible and so far there had been no friction between the two young people. She had met the parents only once and been embarrassed by the wife's inquisitiveness about a job which kept her out so late each night. She had no intention of becoming friendly with them.

She still lived in the sort of dream world in which Michael's eventual bride would regard her new mother-in-law with marvelling devotion.

She had just passed the telephone kiosk (long out of order and heavily vandalised) half-way along the street when she heard a sudden plop and in the same moment felt a violent blow against her right shoulder, which knocked her to the ground.

She hit her head as she fell forward on to the pavement and everything began to swim before her eyes. In the second before she lost complete consciousness, she heard hurriedly retreating footsteps.

CHAPTER 17

The next morning Evesham decided to visit the Metropolitan Police Laboratory on the other side of the river.

He arranged for any telephone calls to be taken and made particular mention of Betsy's name.

He was just about to leave his office when Detective Inspector Cruttenden came on the line. He sounded tired and irritable.

'Thought I better let you know that I'm allowing Huxey to go. Haven't got anything on him.'

'You're satisfied then he had nothing to do with the murder?'

'I suppose so, though questioning him is like trying to communicate with Nelson's Column. Even with an interpreter who can talk to him in sign language.'

'Why'd he disappear?'

'Says he was frightened of Sergeant Wilkley and thought he might try and frame him over Atkins' murder.'

'Where was he hiding?'

'In an attic above one of Ralph Tremler's shops.'

'Then Tremler must have known all the time?'

'Huxey swears he didn't. It isn't the premises where he has his office. It's in a different street altogether.'

'What persuaded you he couldn't have had anything to do with the murder?'

'He has an alibi. He was at hospital having an abscess on his back treated.'

'If he had an alibi, why the hell did he disappear?'

'Because he believed the murder had been committed much later when he didn't have an alibi.'

'I take it you've checked it?'

'Too right I have. Fortunately for him he's not the sort of person anyone forgets. The doctor who attended him, as well as a couple of nurses and a receptionist all recalled his visit. And the hospital records confirm.'

'So what now?'

'I'm off to bed,' Cruttenden said sourly. 'It's taken me the whole bloody night to arrive at this particular lemon.'

'Sleep well! I'll get in touch with you later in the day.'

It seemed clear that Cruttenden didn't expect his Yard colleague to have had any more success than he'd had himself, for he pointedly avoided enquiring about Evesham's own activity or future plans.

Normally the laboratory preferred not to be pestered by visiting officers, apart from those delivering or collecting exhibits. But this was an occasion for a visit rather than a phone call, Evesham had decided. Also the fact that one of the senior liaison officers at the lab was an old friend dating from early days in the force ensured that he would not receive a flea in his ear for making a personal appearance.

'Hello, Tom,' his friend greeted him. 'I was half expecting a visit from you. Run into a brick wall, have you?'

Evesham grinned. 'Is that the only time we get in touch with you?'

'Mostly. Anyway, I rounded up what information we have. Mind you, there's still a lot more work to be done on most of the items, but this is what our boys have reported so far. The bullet extracted from the wall of the magistrate's room is definitely a .22. Unfortunately, it was too far damaged by the impact to tell us anything further. That means it'll never be possible to say from which particular weapon it came.' He turned a page in the folder he was holding. 'Yes, here's quite an interesting point. It could be of significance: on the other hand there may be a simple explanation. Those three letters the magistrate received, with the words cut out and pasted on to the paper. The glue used in the third letter is not the same as that in the first two. Of course it mayn't mean anything more than that the sender had bought a different brand by the time he sent the third letter. But it's a point you may like to think about.'

'It is, indeed,' Evesham said in a thoughtful tone. 'Had all the words and letters been cut from the same newspaper?'

'Can't tell you that yet. I know Mr Langton is still working on the letters. We may know a bit more in a day or so. Trouble is Mr Langton's at the Bailey giving evidence today, so I'm afraid nothing'll be done until he gets back.' He paused. 'Do you know, Tom, there's hardly a soul here some days? They're all out at court, which means their lab work simply piles up. It's the most wasteful system of expert time you can imagine.'

'And all in the cause of justice,' Evesham remarked with a smile.

'Oh, you can mock, Tom, but I happen to be one who thinks our legal system needs a bloody good shake-up. Its principles are mostly O.K., but it was designed for the quill-pen age and doesn't begin to meet modern conditions.'

'You ought to have gone into Parliament, Alec, you'd have had an outlet for your reforming zeal there.'

'But don't you agree with me, Tom?'

'I do and I imagine ninety per cent of the force does as well. However, anything else to tell me?'

'No, that's all for the moment.'

'Right, I'd better be returning to the Yard. My journey's certainly been worthwhile. That information about the two different types of glue provides considerable food for thought.'

On his return he poked his head into the room of the officer who had been taking his calls.

'I'm back, Ken. Any messages?'

'Nothing.'

'No word from Betsy?'

'Not even heavy breathing.'

About fifteen minutes later, however, Ken appeared in Evesham's room holding a newspaper.

'Have you seen a paper this morning?' he asked.

Evesham shook his head. 'Couldn't get one. They were in short supply and sold out by the time I reached the station.'

'There's a bit here about a woman being shot in Fulham last night. It gives her name as Mrs Betsy Luke. Betsy's an unusual name and I just wondered . . .'

'That'll be F Division. I'll call them right away.'

Five minutes later, Evesham had learnt that Mrs Betsy Luke was in Charing Cross Hospital and comfortable after an operation to remove a bullet from her right shoulder. She had been unable to give any description of her assailant as she had been shot from behind and never saw him. It seemed that when she had regained consciousness after a short time she had staggered into the nearest house and the alarm had been raised. The officer to whom Evesham spoke said that someone had clearly been lying in wait for her, probably in a recess by the telephone kiosk. This pointed to someone who knew her movements, but Mrs Luke had, in the officer's opinion, not been as helpful as she could have been in giving the police any sort of lead on this. On the other hand she was obviously still dazed and shocked by her experience and might be readier to talk later on.

As Evesham hurried from the building, he felt sure that Mrs Luke was the Betsy who had phoned Bloomsbury Magistrates' Court the previous afternoon. If so, he was determined that he was going to be the first officer to whom she did do any talking.

It took him twenty minutes to reach the hospital and a further twenty to discover whereabouts Mrs Luke was in the vast building. The receptionist was polite, but unimpressed by his urgent expression as she studied lists and then tried to phone extensions which didn't answer. And when he reached the lift bank it was to see that three of them were already on upward journeys while the fourth was making leisurely downward progress one floor at a time.

Eventually, however, he arrived at the right floor and a passing nurse directed him to a side ward where Betsy Luke, surrounded by screens, was sitting up in bed with a heavily bandaged right shoulder.

'Are you the doctor?' she asked. 'The one who did the operation? The nurse said you'd be looking in this morning.'

'I'm Detective Superintendent Evesham of Scotland Yard, Mrs Luke. Was it you who phoned Bloomsbury Magistrates' Court yesterday afternoon?'

She turned her head away and gazed at the jug of water on the table beside her bed. He saw her bite nervously at her lower lip.

'You were going to call me at the Yard this morning, Mrs Luke,' he went on in a coaxing tone, 'but obviously you couldn't. I believe you have information which may help me in my enquiries. Is that right?'

She turned back and gave him a small nod.

'I can tell you who killed the usher,' she said, in a nervous whisper. She pulled her left hand from beneath the sheet and began to caress the scar on her cheek with a finger. She noticed Evesham watching her. 'Ralph Tremler gave me that,' she added in an almost challenging tone. 'Ten years ago.' She smiled wanly. 'Ralph Tremler and Vic Wilkley; not much to choose between them if you ask me.'

'Are you saying it was one of them?' Evesham said when she seemed to drift away into a reverie.

'Much better if it was. Neither of 'em's any good. No loss to anyone,' she murmured.

She lowered her hand and tucked it beneath the covers.

When she looked back at Evesham, he noticed that her eyes were filled with tears.

'If I talk to you, you must promise never to let Michael know what I've said.'

'Michael?'

'But, of course, you wouldn't know him. Michael's my son. He must never find out the truth. Never.'

'I can't make promises, Mrs Luke, until I hear what you have to tell me, but if Michael's not involved, then I certainly shan't tell him anything.'

'He's just turned fifteen. He's a fine boy.'

'I'm sure.'

She threw Evesham a sidelong glance. 'Are you getting impatient?'

'No. When you're ready to talk, I'll still be here.'

'You see, it's not been an easy decision . . .' Her voice trailed away.

'Someone shot you last night, Mrs Luke. I would think they certainly meant to kill you. Have you any idea who it was?'

Evesham hoped this abrupt reminder of how close she had been to death might jolt her into talking freely.

She stared at him with a puzzled frown. 'No, it was dark. I never saw a soul.'

'But you must have some idea who it was. Why should anyone want to murder you?'

'I can't think. It's a mystery to me.'

Evesham blinked in surprise. She purported to know who killed Reg Atkins, but to have no idea who had shot at her. Perhaps it was the after-effect of the anaesthetic that resulted in her mind functioning in an irrational manner.

'Mrs Luke, why don't you start telling me all you know about the usher's death?' he said, leaning forward to add immediacy to his words.

'He came round. He wanted to see Madeleine. Said he

wanted to talk to her. It was about five o'clock. The evening before he was killed.'

Evesham felt his interest quicken as he realised that Reg Atkins' missing hours were about to be accounted for. Time enough later to discover who Madeleine was, though he thought he could guess.

'I'd never seen him before. There was something odd about him. He was sort of excited and nervous at the same time. I thought perhaps he was another kinky old man. But he kept on saying he only wanted to talk to Madeleine. But after I read about the murder, it set me thinking. And then I called at his home, pretending to be from a newspaper and his wife showed me a snapshot of him and I recognised him at once. It was then I knew what must have happened. Without realising it, it was me he really wanted to talk to. He just assumed it must be Madeleine.' She shook her head. 'The poor little man was barking completely up the wrong tree. And he died without ever knowing . . .'

CHAPTER 18

Philip Smeech and Rachel Ferney were each in a ferment of anxiety, the more so because they had been unable to meet and had been obliged to fall back on the telephone as their only means of communication. Added to which Rachel Ferney now had the feeling that her husband was listening in to every call she made and Philip Smeech had broken out into a cold sweat at the sudden thought that the Ferneys' line might now be tapped. As a result of this fear, he had told her that she must always call him from a public telephone and that he would refrain from phoning her save in a dire emergency.

Soon after her husband had been picked up by the police car deputed to take him to court that morning, she left the house to go and phone Smeech. She very often went out at this hour so that there was nothing to arouse the suspicions of Velma.

It was a relief to get out, the house in Kew having become a prison to her. Donald's presence became more and more oppressive and after he had departed, she found herself dreading the prospect of another visit from Detective Superintendent Evesham. She didn't know how much longer she could withstand him and it was only the awareness that capitulation would spell the end of everything that sustained her. She knew she had to hold out against all his threats and cajoling. He couldn't bully her for the rest of her life, she told herself without much comfort.

'Philip, it's me,' she said, as soon as she heard him answer.

'Where are you speaking from?' he asked nervously.

'A kiosk near Richmond station.'

'A different one from yesterday?'

'Yes. But surely . . .'

'It's best to use a different one each time you call. You weren't followed or anything?'

'No, I'm sure I wasn't. Anyway, once Donald's left, the police lose all interest in the house.'

'Yes, I'm certain it's all right, darling. It's just me being a cautious lawyer again.'

'You make me even more worried when you're like that, Philip,' she said reproachfully.

'I'm sorry, darling. Yours is a much stauncher spirit than mine and it's you who's in the front line at the moment. I do realise all that. It worries me that you're having to shield me. I just hope that everything will soon blow over.'

'But how can it?' she said bleakly.

'We must keep our fingers crossed that the police will become satisfied you can't help them and will take the pressure off.'

If only his tone could have carried a bit more hope and conviction, she reflected miserably.

'How was Donald after he returned from court yesterday?'

'He looked terrible and hardly spoke a word.'

'Did he tell you he'd been shot at?'

'No. I suppose he assumed I knew. I tried to say something appropriate, but he walked out of the room.'

'And this morning?'

'Not even one word. He looked as if he had scarcely slept a wink. I've never seen him like this before. The strain is really beginning to tell on him. He looks as if he might crack up any moment. Oh, Philip, how much longer?' she said in a sudden anguished outburst.

'Just hold on, darling,' he said, urgently. 'It could all be over much sooner than you expect.'

'Do you really think so, Philip?' she asked desperately.

'I wouldn't have said it otherwise. Rely on me a bit longer. I promise not to let you go on suffering like this.'

'But what can you do?'

'Just rely on me,' he repeated.

For some time after she had rung off, he stared out of the window at the court opposite. It was not the thought of the magistrate cracking up under the strain that worried him, but of his wife doing so.

Something had to break soon and he must try and ensure that when it happened, he was nowhere near the fall-out. At all costs he must remain beyond police suspicion.

CHAPTER 19

It was shortly before three o'clock when Evesham slipped into court. The scene was indelibly familiar and yet the atmosphere was subtly different. It was as though the leading participants were going through the motions entirely for the sake of appearance. They were like actors in a play whose performances have become lifeless.

Philip Smeech was addressing Mr Ferney on behalf of a client whose husband had deserted her. He stumbled over his words and looked everywhere save at the magistrate himself. As for Mr Ferney he was leaning back in his chair with an exhausted expression. From time to time he twitched his nose as though one nostril was blocked and glanced at Smeech without interest.

Miss Purton also seemed to be affected by the curious air of lethargy, though she continually cast the magistrate uneasy looks as though any moment expecting another attempt on his life which could encompass her as well.

Inspector Dibben sat wooden-faced in his pen. You could almost hear him counting the days to his retirement, Evesham reflected.

Smeech sat down and started violently when he noticed Evesham at the side of the court. For a second it looked as if he was going to faint, but then like a man in a sleep-walk he bundled his papers into his brief-case and made to depart.

'Magistrate hasn't given judgement yet,' Miss Purton hissed at him.

A few moments later, however, Mr Ferney had made the

necessary maintenance order and the solicitor walked from court looking neither to left nor right.

P.C. Shipling suddenly appeared, followed by Sergeant Wilkley and, lastly, Mr Jude who came hurrying into court red-faced and out of breath.

'Thought I was going to be late,' he muttered to Shipling. 'He's not been waiting, has he?'

'You've timed it to a nicety,' Shipling replied cheerfully.

Evesham went and stood beside the witness box and Sergeant Wilkley smoothed out a large sheaf of notes in readiness to resume battle where it had been broken off the previous day. Everyone awaited Mr Ferney's 'go'.

Instead Mr Ferney said in a dulled tone, 'I regret that I must adjourn. I'm feeling unwell and not able to hear this case further today.'

He rose and hurried from the bench without the usual exchange of bows with counsel and without even a benign glance in the direction of the public gallery.

'Well, that's the bloody limit,' Jude exploded. 'Just because *he's* feeling a bit indisposed, we're treated like dirt. He fixes this afternoon without reference to anyone's convenience apart from his own and now this. I've a good mind to see he's reported to the Lord Chancellor's department.'

'He's been looking under the weather all day,' P.C. Shipling said.

'Then he could have put us off earlier and saved our coming.'

'When am I remanded to?' Sergeant Wilkley chimed in.

'You're not. I'll have to find out. Just hang around a while.'

'Why should I? If the magistrate can't be bothered, I'm not dancing attendance and waiting to hear his pleasure.'

'O.K., bugger off then. But don't complain if someone comes running after you with a warrant.'

The two men glared at each other, before Shipling turned on his heel and left.

Meanwhile Evesham had dashed out of court immediately behind the magistrate. Mr Ferney glanced round as he reached the door of his room, but didn't say anything when he saw who was following him.

'Are you ready to leave now, sir?' Evesham asked. 'The car's outside. It's here early today.'

'I'd like to sit down for a few minutes.'

Evesham followed him into the room and went across to look out of the window.

'The car's waiting,' he said.

'You're in a great hurry to get me out of the building,' Mr Ferney remarked with something of his old acerbity.

'If you're ready, sir,' Evesham went on, as if the magistrate had not spoken.

Mr Ferney hauled himself out of the chair and went over to where his overcoat was hanging. He put it on and reached for his hat.

'What about your brief-case?' Evesham asked as he opened the door.

'I don't carry a brief-case.'

'I noticed you had one when you left yesterday.'

'Just occasionally I have papers to take home.'

Evesham followed him down the stairs which led to the magistrate's entrance. When they reached the car that was parked outside the disused bakery, he opened the back door and then got in beside the magistrate.

'I hadn't realised you were coming, too. I suppose I should feel honoured by the additional protection of a Detective Superintendent.'

'I thought a bit of V.I.P. treatment wouldn't come amiss.'

About ten minutes later, Mr Ferney looked out of the window and frowned.

'This isn't the usual way,' he said suspiciously. When

Evesham said nothing, he went on, 'Where are we going?'

'To Scotland Yard, sir.'

'Scotland Yard? Why am I being taken there?'

'I have some questions I want to put to you about the murder of Reg Atkins.'

CHAPTER 20

'This is an outrage,' Mr Ferney exclaimed angrily. 'You've as good as kidnapped me. Wait until the Lord Chancellor hears about this.'

Evesham said nothing and Mr Ferney sat hunched back glaring ahead of him.

On arrival at Scotland Yard, Evesham quickly led the way to a room set aside for the interview. Detective Inspector Venyon was already there and Evesham formally introduced him. He motioned Mr Ferney to a chair and then sat down to face him across a desk.

'As you're aware, sir, I've been investigating Atkins' death and the events surrounding it and I have reason to believe that you know considerably more than you've told us.'

'Oh? And what precisely do you mean by considerably more?' Mr Ferney asked in his most acidly judicial tone.

'I mean that I think you know who killed him.'

'I've never heard such rubbish.'

'I think it was you yourself who murdered him.'

'I can only believe you've taken leave of your senses, Superintendent. But go on if you must.'

The expected denial but wants to hear more, Evesham reflected not without satisfaction.

'You were aware, of course, that Atkins continued to use the magistrate's entrance against your instructions, particularly on wet evenings. And on the night of his death it was raining hard. You left early, even going to the trouble of telling Miss Purton you were off, which in itself was so unusual that she remembered and mentioned it to me later. Of course it was your way of informing the world that you'd gone home before Atkins left the building. In those circumstances, it was simple for you to return, armed with a bit of lead pipe, and wait for Atkins to emerge. If by any chance he didn't, there'd always be the next day or the one after that.'

Mr Ferney snorted. 'I've come across police blunders before, but this must be the greatest of all time. And an extremely costly one, too, from your point of view. You'll be saying next, I suppose, that I sent myself threatening letters.'

'Only one,' Evesham replied with the air of someone producing a hidden trump. 'The last one. The first two were almost certainly the work of Atkins, but you had to send yourself the third to make it appear your life was still under threat. The laboratory tell me that the glue used to stick on the words of the third letter was different from that on the other two.'

'And you regard that as significant? I've never heard of anything so childish. And how was I supposed to have posted this letter when I didn't leave home the whole of that Saturday, as your own officers can testify?'

'You dined with a friend at Gray's Inn on Friday night. Nothing simpler than to post it on your way home – you were even in the right postal district – and, of course, the box wouldn't have been cleared until the next day, when, as you say, you never went out.'

Mr Ferney made a slight face as if he had swallowed something disagreeable.

'Does your speculation soar into even higher flights of fantasy?'

'Would you like to know why Atkins sent you the threatening letters?'

'You're obviously going to tell me, anyway.'

'It was the backlash of someone you had publicly humiliated and driven to petty revenge.'

'I'd have thought Atkins had much more reason to murder me than the other way round,' Mr Ferney remarked scornfully.

'But his revenge wasn't confined to sending you a couple of threatening letters. He took to following you when you left court to see what you got up to if you didn't go immediately home.'

Mr Ferney's lips seemed to have become uncomfortably dry and he passed his tongue across them, as he cast Evesham a nervous glance.

'He followed you the evening before his death and you spotted him as you came out. He thought you'd gone to visit a prostitute, but you hadn't, had you? You'd gone to make one of your regular calls on her maid, Betsy Luke, the girl who gave birth to your child not long after her sixteenth birthday.'

It seemed to Evesham that the magistrate physically shrank before his eyes. He hung his head, but said nothing.

'I've seen Mrs Luke in hospital this morning, and she has told me how you used to give her money every month and she insisted on your delivering it in person either at her home or at Madeleine's flat as she thought it right you should never forget what you had done to her. It was a monthly reminder of the past which she obviously thought was salutary for you.'

Evesham paused and glanced without sympathy at the slumped figure before him.

'And then yesterday afternoon while I was in your room, Inspector Dibben came in and said that a woman named Betsy was trying to get in touch with me and you realised that the game was almost up. There could only be one Betsy with information to give to the police. And so you embarked on a further murderous enterprise. You took home in your brief-case – remember you had it with you yesterday when you left – the revolver which you had earlier used to simulate an attempt on your own life. By opening one of the side windows, you were able to lean well out and fire through the centre pane. It was a clever idea and well thought out, as you had obviously entered the bakery beforehand and made it appear that was where the marksman had hid himself. Are you willing to tell me what you have done with the revolver?'

But Mr Ferney didn't speak or look up and Evesham went on, 'Your wife has told me that you once had one, though she hadn't seen it for a couple of years or more. I gather from a phone call I made to her just before I arrived at court this afternoon that you went up to your bedroom immediately after dinner last night. That gave you the opportunity of slipping out later, I imagine through your garage to avoid being seen by the officer at the front of the house. I hadn't realised until today that you had a garage at the end of the garden which gave on to a different road.'

Evesham rose. 'We'll now go over to Cannon Row Police Station where you will be charged with the murder of Reg Atkins and the attempted murder of Betsy Luke.'

Rightfully this formality should be completed at the station in which area the murder had been committed, but Evesham felt the case warranted at least this amount of special treatment. Moreover, he realised that he would not be averse to presenting D.I. Cruttenden with the *fait accompli*. He could even be said to be relishing the prospect.

Donald Ferney slowly got up from his chair and gave Evesham a haggard look.

'Satisfy my curiosity on one point,' he said huskily. 'Have you found out who is my wife's lover?'

Evesham shook his head. 'It's no longer relevant to my enquiry.'

In fact, realisation had dawned on him as he watched Philip Smeech's demeanour in court that afternoon. He was surprised that the magistrate had not also guessed. Probably his contempt for the solicitor blinded him. Of course if it was Smeech, it explained Mrs Ferney's desperate anxiety not to reveal his identity and the solicitor's own increasingly strained appearance of late.

Evesham saw no reason, however, to share his deduction with the magistrate. It was probable he would learn soon enough, anyway. But if not, let Mrs Ferney keep her secret.

It seemed ironic that Mr Ferney's trial at the Old Bailey came on several months ahead of Sergeant Wilkley's whose case had to be started all over again before a new magistrate. But eventually the ex-sergeant was convicted by a majority verdict and sent to prison, though not to the same one as Donald Ferney who was by then serving a life sentence.

Evesham used to say afterwards that he'd never known a defendant who gave less trouble. He pleaded guilty at his trial which, as Evesham remarked at the time, was probably the only decent thing he had done in his life.